ANGELA D. SHELTON

Rise of the Y

The Y Chronicles Book 1

First edition

ISBN: 978-1-957649-18-4

Editing by Deirdre Lockhart
Cover art by Clifford Fryman

This book was professionally typeset on Reedsy.
Find out more at reedsy.com

Contents

Acknowledgement	v
Dedication	vi
Chapter 1	1
Chapter 2	15
Chapter 3	22
Chapter 4	31
Chapter 5	39
Chapter 6	49
Chapter 7	59
Chapter 8	69
Chapter 9	78
Chapter 10	88
Chapter 11	98
Chapter 12	108
Chapter 13	117
Chapter 14	126
Chapter 15	136
Chapter 16	146
Chapter 17	155
Chapter 18	163
Chapter 19	172
Chapter 20	181
Chapter 21	189
Chapter 22	197

Chapter 23   206
Chapter 24   214
Chapter 25   227
About the Author   239
Also by Angela D. Shelton   241

Acknowledgement

Creating and launching a novel is a team effort, and I'm grateful for every individual who's been a part of this journey. A big shoutout to the members of ACFW and Word Weavers Critique Groups—your feedback as beta readers has been invaluable. Huge thanks to my editor, Deirdre Lockhart, who always keeps me on track. Clifford Fryman, my fantastic cover designer—your patience is a godsend.

I can't thank my launch team enough for spreading the word about my book. Interested in being part of the excitement for my next YA novel? Click the link to join my launch team: https://forms.gle/Fqpyn6vWGTfhhjfB6.

Launch team members for this novel included: Loretta Gilstrap, Patricia Harris, Megan Short, Sam Stokes, and Lauren Thell.

Dedication

To the radiant memory of my mother,

Your love was the unwavering beacon that guided my journey through the labyrinth of words. With every page I penned, I felt the gentle brush of your encouragement, and in every story I shared, I saw your eyes gleam with pride. You read each book, each line, as if you were embarking on the adventure with me. Though you're no longer here to turn the pages, your spirit dances between the lines, and your voice whispers in every word. This book, and every story that follows, is a testament to your belief in me.

Always and forever, your legacy thrives in the tales I tell.

Chapter 1

Lexi Verity's eyes burned. She twisted her watch into view. Well past midnight. Flipping her school tablet shut, she gave up for the night. *If you haven't figured it out yet, it's doubtful more cramming will help.*

Ratios of fertilizer to water, ideal growing temperatures for the different plants, and the nutrient levels of various flora classifications swirled in her tired brain. Life was so unfair. If the Imperium had permitted her to choose her career path, she'd already have the details down pat. Of course, if she'd started studying sooner, that would have helped too.

The question looming over her now was whether she'd have the guts to put her plan into action. It didn't take her massive IQ to calculate the potential outcomes of tomorrow's test. If she stuck to the plan the Imperium laid out for her years ago, she'd wear the same white uniform of the upper-class Administration she'd worn her entire life. Her life would be predictable, comfortable, and affluent, especially compared with what others could expect.

She nibbled the corner of a protein bar, then stared at it. What a shame they took perfectly tasty vegetables and turned them into boring slabs. Healthy? Of course. Efficient? Definitely. How she'd love to snack on fresh chickpeas instead of the same processed blocks she had since she was old enough to chew.

Though, she *might* get the life she'd daydreamed about ever since visiting the greenhouses on a school field trip when she was five. She could still remember her awe over the plants that sprang out of the hydroponic systems as if by magic. And those videos they played, showing the time-lapse photos of the seeds germinating, then growing and fruiting—wow. They'd even given each of them a fresh green bean to taste. Bliss. It would be a dream to work in the greenhouses, caring for the vegetables, and soaking in the sun every day. Talk about the ultimate work assignment. She laid her tablet aside, closed her eyes, and drifted off into a troubled sleep.

The scent and sizzle of bacon in a skillet woke her. At least she thought it was bacon, but that couldn't be. Was it possible to smell in a dream?

She cracked her eyelids open and peered out from under the pillow she'd burrowed beneath. Their micro-apartment hid very little, and her mother's thin frame, white uniform, and long blond hair came into focus as she stood in the kitchen—cooking.

Lexi lifted her head and sniffed. Grease. Her stomach growled. "Mom? Is that what I think it is?"

Her mother turned, her smile glowed as bright as the sun. "Morning, sleepyhead. You ready for your big day?"

Ugh. Why did Mom have to remind her? Lexi had wrestled in her dreams all night. In her sleep, she'd lived every potential, horrible outcome, nightmare upon nightmare. Now, the day had arrived—no way to avoid it. "Do I have a choice?"

Her mother shrugged. Not reassuring. "You've got the choice of bacon and eggs or the usual protein bar for breakfast.

Does that help?"

Lexi inhaled every ounce of breath her lungs could hold, savoring the rare treat. "Kinda?"

Her mother's tinkling laugh soothed Lexi's nervous tension. "Come on. Out of bed. Enjoy as much of your birthday surprise as you can before you go to school."

Her foldaway mattress slid into the couch after Lexi tossed her pillow into a side-table drawer. She should have at least flung the covers back into place to "make" the bed before she put it away, but Mom wouldn't say anything. Not today.

Lexi walked a few feet across the room and snuggled up to her mother's side by the stove. Her mom's scent enveloped her. Floral, like spring flowers from the rooftop garden.

Mom closed her favorite cookbook and tucked it under her arm. Soon, she'd walk the short distance to her bedroom to put it away before they ate, an odd daily routine. Mom was a skilled cook on the few occasions they had actual food to prepare. Usually, they ate the protein bars mass-produced in the Imperium's ovens.

Fresh vegetables were a rare treat. Animal proteins were even more so. The Imperium decided years ago that providing fresh foods resulted in waste. Humans squandered too much, so all foodstuffs went into the bland but healthy bars. Still, every morning, Mom read her recipe book, planning for special occasions—like today. Mom had even written in it once, making notes.

A door opened, and Nana slipped out, clicking it shut behind her. With a mischievous grin, she closed the gap between herself and Lexi and wrapped Lexi in a bear hug. "How's my birthday girl?"

Nana's silky hair tickled Lexi's nose. "Morning, Nana. How's

Gramps?"

A frown crinkled Nana's face as she pulled away. "He's worn out from the doctor's visit yesterday. I already called off work for him so he can sleep in."

Gramps would never have stayed in bed, especially today, if he felt well enough to be in the kitchen. A weight settled into Lexi's stomach.

"Come on. No sad faces this morning." Nana patted Lexi's arm. "We're celebrating."

Right. The bacon must have set the family budget back. So Lexi rubbed her hands together and forced a cheery tone. "Let's eat."

Her father wandered in and took a seat at the table, scrolling through messages on his tablet. His dark hair lay slicked back, as neat as his spotless, white government uniform. He looked up but didn't smile as Lexi joined him. "I see the celebration has already begun. Happy birthday, Lexi."

"Thank you."

Cool and efficient, her father had never been the most engaged parent. Somehow, she couldn't spit out the word *Dad,* but it felt stupid to call him *Father.*

He squeezed her hand. "Last birthday together, unless you're assigned to engineering. If you don't get in there, it won't be long, and you'll have a mate and a child of your own."

Why did he always have to ruin everything? Her stomach tightened around the weight already there. The bacon didn't seem as tempting any longer. "I'd better get my shower."

"No." Mom slid the pan off the burner, lifted the five strips from it, and spread them onto a plate. "We need to eat while it's warm. Can't waste your birthday treat. Everybody, sit."

She padded to her bedroom, her cookbook under her arm,

while they situated themselves around the oak table. The wooden top took up a significant portion of their small apartment. With five family members, the sixth chair seemed unnecessary. They rarely had a visitor, but Mom liked the symmetry.

The pullout couch across the room had an L-shaped wing to allow them to sit together during the infrequent Imperium newscasts. Along with the kitchen area, the dining room completed their open-concept space. Two bedrooms, a bathroom, and the living area. Less than four hundred square feet created the only home Lexi had ever known, though her parents had started in a one bedroom as every Imperium couple did.

On her way back from the bedroom, Mom moved the plate of bacon to the table and set it next to a steaming bowl of scrambled eggs. Nana placed salt and pepper shakers in the center. They so seldom needed seasonings that the containers' presence looked festive.

"Today's the big day." Dad scooped two spoonsful of eggs onto his plate before passing the bowl to Lexi. "You ready for the test?"

Test. The worst four-letter word, and she'd heard plenty of bad ones whispered between the other girls in school. "Ready as I'll ever be."

His eyebrows rose as he focused on her. "You should eat at least half a protein bar too." He waved at her plate. "The bar has all the nutritional value your body needs to be in top form for the exam."

"Gunner, leave her be." Mom glared at him with a forkful of egg halfway to her mouth. "The test isn't everything. Let her enjoy her special day."

"Yes, it *is everything*." He jammed his utensil at his wife. "Today determines whether she's assigned to engineering in Administration or gets transferred to one of the other places. You know what that means."

Lexi might vomit. The salty bacon and eggs turned to sawdust on her tongue. The living-quarters assignment was part of the job package. The Imperium valued efficiency above all else. They'd never place her in housing devoted to Administration employees if she didn't qualify for a job in the building.

"Let's not argue." Nana clucked. "We don't want to stress Lexi anymore today. Right?"

Right. Enough already. Lexi's breaths grew shorter, and her chest constricted. Why did she feel as if it were her responsibility to end the tension between her parents? "I'm sure I'll do fine, and whatever job I'm assigned will be for the best."

Nana patted Lexi's hand from across the table. "It'll be great. You'll see."

Dad swallowed the last of his breakfast. "Hmph. Eat the protein bar." He pushed back his chair, the metal legs grating against the bamboo floor. "I've got a meeting first thing. Need to head out."

He went into their bedroom, then emerged moments later, still clinging to his ever-present electronic work tablet. After he patted Lexi on the head and kissed Mom's cheek, he opened the front door. "Happy birthday, Lexi. Do your best, and you'll do us proud."

The door shut behind him, and the tension in her body eased. He'd be angry if he knew what she'd planned. A peek at her wristwatch told her she needed to get moving. "Thanks for breakfast, Mom. It was amazing."

Sadness tinged the smile Mom gave her. "You're welcome, sweetie. Remember, your father only wants the best for you, but no matter what, this test doesn't define you."

Lexi held back a derisive laugh. The test *did* define her. That was the whole point—to determine what job she'd slave at for the rest of her life. Once the Imperium decided her career, they'd choose her best genetic match. The thought of marriage, of the unknown *him*, twisted her stomach's knot even tighter.

She rushed through her brief, tepid shower. The Imperium didn't permit the waste of water or electric resources, even if it was a special day. After toweling off, she wriggled into her white, shapeless, Administration jumpsuit and dragged her brunette hair back into an efficient ponytail.

Hazel eyes stared at her from the mirror above the sink. They glinted faintly blue in the bright lights. Too bad, she didn't have either her mother's blue or her father's green irises. Hers changed color based on what she wore or what the lighting she was in. Never the same.

She wanted to be like her eyes—always changing. But change wasn't valued in the Imperium. It was like living with a herd of automatons. Follow in line, don't make a fuss, and never disturb the routine.

If only she'd lived in the time before the Collapse and the war. Nana's stories from when she was a girl were colorful and exciting. People chose what to eat, how to dress, and who to love. Lexi would have adored that life. With a sigh, she whispered, "Happy birthday to me."

"Lexi, you need to get going." Mom's voice from beyond the bathroom door jolted Lexi. "You're going to be late."

Time to face the day. "Yes, ma'am."

Lexi scurried out of the apartment after a quick kiss to both Nana and Mom. She hadn't made it halfway down the hall toward the bridge when a door opened and closed behind her.

The snobbish twang of her nosy neighbor, Courtney Blakeslee, called out. "Wait up. I'll walk with you."

Ugh. No thank you. Was she far enough ahead to make-believe she hadn't heard?

Footsteps hurried behind her. "Big day, huh?"

Nope. Can't get away. Dad would have her hide if she wasn't polite. Politics were too important in the Administration section. Without a glance toward Courtney, Lexi sped up as she talked. "Yup. Big day. Don't want to be late."

"Right, work exams, but you know how thin the walls are, right? It's your birthday too. Congrats."

Courtney was the last person Lexi wanted to celebrate with. "Thanks. Happens every year."

They arrived at the crossover bridge, offering their first glimpse of the weather. The dark sky roiled with rain-filled clouds. From the moment they stepped into the long vein pumping people from the living apartments to the Administration building, Lexi knew she'd rush across. The storm generated wind gusts strong enough to make the bridge sway.

Engineers had designed the connection to give and take with the gales, but the sensation set her on edge. Knowing the safety feature existed didn't always equate to her brain accepting the movement was secure.

Courtney stopped midway across, overlooking the ground three stories below. "I sure hope everyone does well today. I'd hate to be one of those poor people down there. Can you imagine life without a job?"

Lexi could imagine. The Favela was less of a community than

a pit of despair. She'd begged Mom to take her down one time to give out protein bars to the homeless. The hopelessness on all their faces had been more than she could bear. She'd never asked to go again.

That trip was the first time Lexi had seen the Y tag of the rebellion. Rebels had etched the unusual symbol on at least a quarter of the buildings. She'd asked her parents and grandparents about Y, but the only thing any of them would admit was the group was anti-Imperium. Not one detail more.

The space between Lexi and Courtney had widened as Lexi continued moving while Courtney gazed downward. The moment Lexi's feet left the bridge, she waved to her neighbor. "Gotta go. Later."

By the time she reached her learning pod, her breaths came in gasps. She slapped her palm on the screen to gain access to the system. One minute late. The computer permitted a two-minute punctuality window, so the screen shaded yellow, not the dreaded crimson hue that signaled a demerit.

Across the aisle, the platinum swish of hair drew her to her best friend, Aponi Liam. Lexi loved her name's meaning—butterfly warrior. It fit perfectly with Aponi's platinum blonde hair and electric-blue eyes.

Aponi winked. "You made it. I am *so* ready for this. Who knows, I might meet *him* this week."

The Imperium's anthem wafted out of the pod's headphones. Lexi positioned them over her ears as the first of the four mottos scrolled across her screen. The system would listen for her to parrot them along with the rest of the class, so she muttered into the microphone.

Unity above all else.

Hard work lifts us all.

A young Imperium is a thriving Imperium.

One marriage—many children.

Aponi spoke the words along with her. When they'd finished, Aponi grinned and gave Lexi the thumbs-up signal. How could their views on the test be such opposites?

A robotic voice interrupted Lexi's musing. "Your exam will commence in one minute."

Aponi drew a heart in the air, hugged her arms to her chest, and sighed.

Lexi shook her head. Her friend insisted on the ridiculous notion of falling madly in love with the genetically perfect guy the Imperium chose for her. As if the system cared whether affection factored into the match. Last time Aponi had voiced her excitement about the upcoming nuptials, Lexi scowled. "You'll probably get hooked up to some fifty-year-old politician who's afraid he'll lose his apartment because his kids graduated."

The possibility was all too real. She'd heard of a girl who graduated a few years ago being assigned to a high-level Imperium council member when his second wife died before she got pregnant. The guy had to have been fifty—at a minimum. Lexi shivered.

Only those just married or with children got apartments. Those who didn't get pregnant after their first year of wedlock or whose children had grown and moved out, lived dormitory-style unless their children took them in. The Imperium only permitted one additional bedroom per child, so not everyone took in their elders. Lexi slept on the couch so her grandparents could have a bedroom in their tiny place instead of being stuck in the dorms. No matter who they mated her to, he'd better be prepared for a multigenerational household.

She'd sleep on the bathroom floor to keep her grandparents and parents in her marital apartment. It would be tight, but surely, others had done it before. But she didn't want to think about that now.

Aponi stuck out her tongue. "You don't have a romantic bone in your body."

A warning sounded in the headphones. The doors that would seal them in and prevent cheating lowered across the entrances. "Exam commencing. Please turn your attention to the screen."

They waved to each other and gave the thumbs-up. Aponi's face shone with hopeful anticipation. Lexi's stomach clenched. This was it.

She'd been in school since the age of four with the goal of each class to prepare her for this one test. One hundred questions would determine the rest of her life. Aptitude assessments had narrowed the field throughout the years, and a career in engineering was her most likely outcome. That is—if she kept with their plan for her career.

If today's results reflected such, she'd have two more years of school, then be stuck in the same building where her parents had lived. With her father's pull, he'd get her assigned to the same floor, maybe even the same apartment she'd always lived in if he called in every favor he'd ever tucked away for an emergency. Then her new husband could join her on the pullout couch. That wouldn't last long though if she didn't get pregnant fast. Two bedrooms were normally reserved for those with children, and as soon as she graduated, she was no longer a child. Her father's status would only get them so far. She clutched the hem of her sleeve, her dull uniform the clothing of Administration. If she played along, she'd live in this bland world—with no relief—until the day she could no longer work.

An electronic voice interrupted her thoughts as the screen flashed the first question. "Please begin."

If she did well, she'd follow in her parents' footsteps. She'd know no other world than the one she'd lived in now. Was that what she wanted—the same white existence with an assigned mate who was most likely just as boring?

The voice repeated. "Please begin."

The answer took hold of her with a sensation as if she'd been filled with helium and was now lighter than air, as if the solution had set her free.

No. She wanted something else, and there was only one way to get it. She had to blow the test for engineering in just the right way to be assigned to the Green building the Imperium assigned the Growers to. That was her only way out.

"Please begin."

It was time for a new life. The years of white had to end.

The test contained a section for each of the job categories. Since they'd geared her training toward engineering, that would be her first section while her brain was fresh. She answered the first question with the wrong answer. Lexi read some inquiries to ensure wrong answers while providing correct responses to others. Years of educational grooming put her in a position where she could waltz into an administrative job. She needed to ensure it didn't look as if she'd thrown the test. But how many wrong questions would it take to guarantee a different role while not losing her spot in the aboveground community?

Once she was through the first section, she relaxed and sped through the next three parts related to jobs and buildings she didn't care about. She should have researched those possibilities before the test. Too late now. She'd burned through half the questions faster than she'd imagined possible. Then the Grower section came up. This part she needed to ace. Sweat beads popped up on her forehead as she thought through each line and put forth her best effort.

After she answered that section's last question, she slowed to peek at the pod across the aisle. Aponi's finger rested on her chin while her tongue poked out of the side of her mouth, indicating her best friend was deep in thought. Aponi's schooling had prepared her for a low-level administrative job that wouldn't require further education. There was no uncertainty she'd ace the test. Losing her friend would be difficult. If Lexi were no longer in the same building, it would be harder to keep the friendship alive.

It didn't matter anymore. Aponi wanted nothing more than the Imperium's plan. For years, she'd dreamed it would be an exciting adventure in romance. Why, Lexi couldn't understand.

She returned her attention to her screen, powered through the rest of the exam, then took a deep breath before answering the last question. This was it. One final press on the screen and the system would assign her a career.

If the profession required more education, she'd be back in the same pod tomorrow for two more years of school. If she'd had enough training, the Imperium would provide her with a uniform and the place to report the following day. Within days, the system would assign her a mate and their new living quarters. All that would remain would be to say goodbye to everyone and everything she'd ever known. *If* she'd executed her plan correctly.

With her finger millimeters from the screen, she closed her eyes, then pressed.

A robotic voice spoke. "You have completed the exam. Please hold for your results."

Her heart hammered. The fear of what waited for her on the screen kept her eyes squeezed tight until the voice came to life once again. "Lexi Verity, the Imperium has assigned you to Reclamation. Please report for duty to the Brown tower, basement level, tomorrow morning at eight a.m. Your mate and apartment assignments will be delivered to your current address within seventy-two hours."

Reclamation? What was that? Lead settled in the pit of her stomach, and her heart pounded even harder. Her quick breaths pulled her toward the edge of hyperventilation. This wasn't how it was supposed to go.

The girls' learning pod door slid up. Her days of education had ended. Seventy-two hours. Just three short days from now, she'd be out of her parents' home, out of the White towers, and mated.

Lexi peeked into Aponi's pod, waved goodbye, then walked on unsteady legs. Her entire body shook over what the next three days held for her. *What have I done?*

Chapter 2

The walk home was a march to Lexi's own execution. Her breakfast rose in her throat, burning her esophagus with its reflux. For what had to be the hundredth time this morning, she wished she'd eaten the protein bar instead of the bacon.

Her skin crawled with her paranoia. Every person she passed was eyeing her in suspicion as if they knew she no longer belonged in the Administration buildings. After all, she didn't. This was no longer her home. She now belonged to Reclamation.

When she approached the connection bridge, the tension in her body urged her to sprint to release some of it. She needed to get home, away from the prying stares she imagined bored through her.

The windows on the bridge remained dark from the raging storm. From the moment her foot touched the floor of the swaying connection, she sprinted until she saw something on the opposite side. She stopped, gulping in air with her hands on her knees, as her brain took in the mark.

Purple spray paint dripped down the glass. Someone with an artistic flare had tagged the window with a Y designed to look like a bird. The damp image still fresh enough, the chemical scent tinted the air. Lexi checked behind her, then toward the apartment building. The culprit had vacated the area.

An alarm sounded, and a strobe light flashed over cameras at either end of the bridge. She continued past the tagged window and reached the other side as men in yellow maintenance worker uniforms rode out of the Administration building on a cart. One of them called to her. "Citizen, stand and be recognized."

They didn't think she'd been the one to deface the window, did they? She froze in place, grateful she'd stepped off the swaying bridge and into the solid building.

A man with spiked black hair exited the cart and walked to the camera Lexi stood beneath. His grim stare brooked no shenanigans. "Identify yourself."

She placed her palm on the detection pad of his tablet. "I'm Lexi Verity. I live here in the Administration building." He didn't need to know about her new assignment.

The pad flashed green, and her picture appeared along with her data for the worker to review. After a quick study of the screen, he nodded to the camera above her. "Did you spray-paint the camera and the window?"

Above her, the same purple paint covered the camera lens. Her heart might beat out of her chest soon, and a wave of dizzy nausea hit her. "No. I–I wouldn't. It was like that when I got here."

Spiky Hair turned to the bald guy who'd already cleaned the purple mark off the window. "Check the other camera feed."

Bald Guy picked up his own tablet and tapped. "Got it."

Spiky Hair did likewise on his own handheld and brought up the feed for the camera she stood under. The angle he held the tablet allowed her a view. In the video replay, citizens crossed over the bridge, caricatures of real people at high speed. Then came a lull in the traffic. An arm holding a can rose into view. A purple cloud misted the lens until it went dark. Spiky hollered back to Bald Guy, "Nothing on this one."

Bald Guy held up a thumb. "She's clear on this end. Her hand was empty when she entered on this side. We need a third camera in the middle. I lose her from view when she's a little more than halfway across."

After Spiky Hair switched his tablet off, he tossed it into the maintenance cart. "You can go now, miss."

Part of Lexi wanted to bolt for home, but she jiggled in place. "Why would someone tag the window like that? What does it mean?"

Spiky's glower conveyed more than the terse response. "You can go now."

She didn't waste another second. Instead, she dashed toward the safety of her apartment. By the time she raised her palm to the security pad outside their door, her hand trembled as the light scanned it.

The screen turned green, the lock clicked open, and she entered what was now officially her former home. In three days, she'd have her new one. Emotions overwhelmed her. The terror of the unknown mixed with the excitement of new opportunities. She needed to research Reclamation. It could be even better than the greenhouse—or worse than Administration. Focused on studying the greenhouse, she'd neglected all other areas. Her family would be angry at first. They'd all have to move to the Reclamation towers. But they'd get over it once they realized she'd take them all in at her new home—right? Everyone except her father. He might move into the dorms in Administration despite any offers she made.

Silence greeted her. Mom, Dad, and Nana were all at work. She didn't see Gramps in the living area. For good or bad, she needed to share the test results with someone. Her secret rebellion would now be public news, and not sharing it ate at her sanity. A rustle came from her grandparents' bedroom.

She tapped on Gramps's bedroom door and whispered. "Gramps. You awake?"

No response. She twisted the knob and opened the door an inch to whisper again. "Gramps? It's Lexi."

A snuffle sounded from where Gramps lay, his face as pale as the white sheets he rested between. When he didn't respond, she closed the door. She'd have to wait for Nana or Mom to get home to share her news.

After a click at the front of the apartment, Dad strode in and slammed the door behind him. His eyes found hers, and the fire in them burned into her. "What. Did. You. *Do*?"

He advanced while she backed away.

She'd never seen him so angry—almost unhinged. He couldn't know somehow, could he? "I... *what*?"

He waved his tablet at her, then jabbed a finger at the lit screen. "*Reclamation*? You've been on target for engineering your entire school career. You could have gone higher than I have. Instead, you've been assigned to *Reclamation*?"

A fire flared in her chest. This was *her* life. *Her* choice. "Yes. Reclamation. *Not* Administration. I want my *own* life. Not yours."

His advance stopped only inches from her, invading her personal space.

He leaned down until all she could see were his black pupils. "You're fortunate I've got a few favors I can pull. I'm getting you retested. Until then, you'll work in Reclamation during

18

the day, and you'll work with a tutor at night."

How dare he. She pushed upward on her toes so he had to back up an inch to avoid her nose smashing into his. Her fists balled, and she growled. "I'm seventeen now—legally an adult. You can't tell me what to do."

A bark of laughter exploded from him. He stepped away and cut one hand through the air. "Watch me."

He stormed out of the apartment, the door banging behind him.

Erupting, she grabbed a pillow off the couch and flung it at the door. "I'm seventeen!"

The act wasn't enough to assuage her. The fire continued to flow as she yanked the pillows and then the cushions off the sofa, hurling them in all directions. She screamed out her frustration. When nothing remained but the pullout frame, she flopped down on it, spent.

The metal bars bruised the back of her thighs. *Stupid couch.*

"Feel better now?" Gramps stood in his bedroom doorway, his face white, his limbs trembling.

Her stomach clenched. "Sorry. I didn't mean to wake you."

He shuffled toward her, holding onto the counter for support.

She scrambled up, gathered the cushions and pillows, and put them into place, along with an extra pillow to support him. Then she took his arm and helped him the last few feet to the sofa.

His legs shook as he settled in before he patted the seat beside him.

She let out a sigh. *Time for a lecture. I deserve one.*

The twinkle in his eye matched the smirk on his lips. "Reclamation, huh? I get why you wouldn't want to work in engineering, don't want to stay in the Administration building, but did you have to blow the test *that* much?"

The pressure of the test, the graffiti incident, and her father's anger had built enough tension to keep her awake for the rest of her life. His grin popped the stress bubble enveloping her, and she chuckled. Once she started, the floodgates opened, and she laughed until tears flowed. Gramps joined her, but he ended in a spate of coughs.

She wiped her tears, got a glass of water, and handed it to him.

As he sipped, his cough subsided. "Seriously. I'll love you no matter what. Is Reclamation what you *really* want?"

That question had swirled in her brain since the computer read out her assignment. All jobs were important to the city. Every citizen's work mattered. That was the mantra the Imperium preached every day. But Reclamation? At least she'd wear brown instead of the nothingness of white. "I'm not sure, Gramps. I was trying for the greenhouse. But anything's better than Administration."

A notification alarm sounded from Nana and Gramps's bedroom. He sighed. "Run and get that for your old gramps, will you?"

"You got it." She pressed a kiss to his cheek, trotted into the bedroom to retrieve his tablet, and handed it to him. "It's odd they're sending a notification when you're off. It could've waited until you're feeling better."

He shrugged and pulled up the message that sent out an intermittent chirp. His eyes grew wide. "We gotta call Nana." His pale cheeks splotched crimson, and his eyebrows rose while he read the message out.

" 'Congratulations, Imperium grants you early retirement

via lottery draw. Transfer orders to Solitude to follow.' " He lowered the tablet, letting it clatter to the wooden side table. "Nana and I are retiring before sixty."

She flopped beside him. She'd heard of early retirement being awarded, but never thought it could happen to her grandparents. Wanting to be close, she wormed against him until he wrapped his arm around her. "You… you're leaving?"

The thought of her family being available, even coming with her after she moved, comforted her since she'd decided to get out of the Administration towers. But when citizens retired, they moved to a separate city, miles south. Communication rarely occurred between the municipalities.

While the stories of sunny pools, lush gardens, and relaxation were plentiful, she'd known no one who'd ever returned, even for a visit, from Solitude. She wouldn't see them again.

He leaned his head down to rest on hers. "We've been fortunate your parents took us in. Nana and I have been a part of your life. Watching you grow up was more than I could have wished for, sweet girl."

Tears threatened to overflow, and she swiped at them with her sleeve. She'd rather be angry than brokenhearted. He was right. Not everyone got to have relationships with their grandparents. She'd been lucky. Her words were moist as she worked to swallow her tears. "I don't want you to go."

A fit of coughs kept him from speaking. Then his next comment brought no comfort. "I know. Nana and I don't want to leave either, but it's time."

She wanted to do something—*anything*—to stop them from going away. What stupid rules. Yes, the city couldn't hold the growing population, but they shouldn't force people to move just because they were old. It was wrong—just plain wrong.

Chapter 3

The blare and vibration of Lexi's watch shocked her awake. Her sleep-deprived eyes struggled to focus on the blurred numbers. Administration personnel reported to work in the morning, but not in the dark. Why did Reclamation have to start at five a.m.? What couldn't wait until a reasonable hour?

Perhaps her father had the right idea to retest. She could pretend she'd had a migraine or some other ailment. She peered at the brown uniform draped across the arm of the couch and shook her head. "Don't be such a wimp."

When the package arrived last night, Mom said the outfit made her eyes look the color of moss. Lexi had been thrilled the jumpsuits were anything except white. For the first time in her life, she'd leave their apartment in clothing with color. A smile tugged at her lips. She'd be out of the Administration building today for more than a brief trip. She was going to see the world!

Her parents' bedroom door opened. Mom shut it behind her before whispering, "Morning."

Guilt wormed into Lexi's happy thoughts. She rolled out of bed and tossed the blankets into place before lifting the mattress into the couch. "You didn't have to get up. It's too early."

Mom helped put the cushions in place, then plopped onto one, drawing Lexi down beside her. "I wouldn't miss my baby's first day of work. Especially when I know we've only got two more mornings together."

What a gut punch. Everyone knew the possibility she'd move out when she turned seventeen. She'd only stay until the age of nineteen if she'd been assigned a high-level Administration position, such as engineering, that would require an additional two years of school. Most education ended at seventeen.

Lexi's throat tightened, and her words came out strangled. "I know you love living here in Administration, but I can bring you and Dad with me."

Mom's arm wrapped around Lexi's shoulders. Then she lifted Lexi's chin to face her. "Today isn't the day for worrying about housing. This one is for adventure."

So true. *What was I thinking?* Who knew what she'd find out there on the other side of the Administration building walls? She'd been out of the twin towers on the rare occasion, but didn't know much about the other buildings or the people who lived in them. Regardless, she'd be out of the sterile white. "I'd better get changed. Don't want to be late on my first day."

The dirt-brown fabric, rough against her skin, would hold up to most physical activity. This cloth wasn't made for office work. She secured her hair into a ponytail and stared at her reflection. With a jab at the mirror, she straightened to her full height. "*You* are going to have an amazing day."

Excitement tingled in her veins. At least, she'd be up and moving instead of stuck behind a desk. Who knew, she might even dig in real dirt instead of the hydroponic medium in the rooftop gardens.

Nana had told her tales of when people planted gardens in the soil. A time when people lived in individual houses and had grass lawns outside their front doors instead of hallways to other apartments. What if Reclamation put her to work in the greenhouse on their roof? They'd have one similar to the one on the building she'd grown up in. She'd indulge in sunshine every day.

Unable to contain her excitement, she set off.

She never had a reason to push the elevator button for the subbasement. People went to the lowest level to ride the tram between buildings. Air bridges connected the living and work towers, but the tramway took passengers between the various building classes. It was the only way to get to Reclamation— her new home.

When the elevator door opened, she joined a group in various uniforms who waited for the tram. Her own brown blended well with green, yellow, orange, and even one black-clad Freedom Force officer not yet in full uniform. A soldier stood on a raised platform and scanned the crowd, a rifle in his arms, legs spread in a stance of readiness.

The sight made her stomach squirm. This dreary, cement-walled station was so different from the Administration building's bright, white environment. The surrounding faces didn't have the smiles of morning greetings. No one spoke.

Perhaps the guard had others on edge as well.

The tram arrived, and she followed the crowd through the door. Before she sat, the door slid shut. The vehicle took off, and a feminine voice came over a loudspeaker. "Next stop, Yellow."

Tunnel walls sped by. Lights every few yards provided flashes of illumination as the tram passed. Though the speed prevented a thorough inspection, Lexi thought she saw a recognizable symbol among the spray-painted tags. A purple Y-shaped bird like the one on the air bridge.

Someone risked a lot to put those tags out during the night. If the Freedom Force caught them, the Imperium could banish them from all the buildings. Their punishment could be homelessness in the Favela. Or worse.

Why would anyone take that risk? What could they hope to gain from defacing property?

At the Yellow stop, two people disembarked. The overhead voice made another announcement as the doors closed. "Next stop, Brown."

This was it—her new world. She'd only take the tram back and forth for two days. Then she'd have her own apartment in the Reclamation building. Well... hers and her new mate's. But that thought was best left for another day. Forced marriage... A shiver ran up her arm.

When the doors slid open again, the scent of something rotten, mixed with a strong antiseptic, wafted into the tram. Her nose revolted as she walked onto the platform. A few other brown-uniformed passengers also disembarked, and she fell in line behind them.

A tap on her shoulder captured her attention. A guy about her age stood in a brown jumpsuit as clean and pressed as her own. Curly brown hair accentuated emerald eyes and a strong jawline. At least six inches taller than she was, he looked down as he walked beside her. "You look new here. It's my first day too. Want to tag along? I'm Ethan."

His eyes drew her in. Their color reminded her of the rooftop garden greenery—fresh and alive. What were the chances the Imperium would match her to someone as gorgeous as him? *Stop dreaming, girl. It doesn't work that way.* He'd be at the top of her list of guys to get to know if she had the choice. "I'm Lexi. That would be great. It'd be nice to know at least one person."

The parade of brown uniforms ended at a checkpoint where workers placed their palms on the scanner to clock in. With each scan, the green glow passed someone through. When she placed her own palm on the screen, it flashed orange. A burly man with dirty-blond hair, beefy hands, and a tablet stepped up to her. Her picture came up on the man's screen. "Lexi Verity, you're assigned to my area. Step to the side and wait for the rest of your team members."

She moved to the opposite wall. Her new friend placed his palm on the scanner. It flashed orange, and the supervisor pointed to her. "Ethan Cabot. Please join Ms. Verity."

Ethan grinned as he moved beside her. "Looks like we're on the same team. Even better."

The day looked more hopeful. Not only was he friendly, but he was also easy on the eyes. She returned the smile—her first-day jitters calmed.

The last of five recruits joined the group along the wall when the starting bell chimed. The supervisor faced them. "My name is Mr. Douglas Taylor. You can call me Mr. Taylor, boss, or sir. I expect you to arrive before the bell chimes and be at your stations, ready to go when it sounds. Hard work lifts us all."

Mr. Taylor stared at them as if expecting a response. When none came, his gaze hardened, and he repeated himself. "Hard work lifts us all."

Ethan pulled his shoulders back and parroted. "Hard work lifts us all."

Lexi joined in the echoes of the remaining newbies.

Satisfied they'd all responded, Mr. Taylor continued. "You are now members of the reclamation team. Here we correct the faults of those who came before us, at least as much as we can. For generations, humans wasted everything. Spoiled with abundant food, technology, and water, they threw resources into mountain-sized piles called landfills."

Though Lexi's grandmother told her tales of huge mounds of disposed items, Mr. Taylor surely exaggerated. No one would casually throw away resources, but she wouldn't argue on her first day.

He continued. "Our task is to deconstruct those hills and recover precious resources. Other teams will then recycle the resources into usable materials. It will take time for you to learn what is of value and what can't be reclaimed. Use your monitors to research any items you are unfamiliar with. Questions?"

So many thoughts bombarded her brain she didn't know where to start. A glance at the rest of her new team showed none of them had moved, but stood at attention, waiting for instructions. Not wanting to be the one clueless, she kept her mouth shut.

With a nod, Mr. Taylor walked toward a steel door. An overpowering odor assaulted her nose as he tugged it open. He waved them through. "Let's get you suited up."

They filed in, and he paused at a line of narrow cabinets with scanner pads. "Choose an available locker with a yellow light. Your palm will open it and assign it to you for the day. At the end of your shift, you are to retrieve any belongings so the locker is available for the next shift. It also contains both a clean suit and a gas mask. Put them on and follow me."

The brown suit inside the locker she chose fit loosely over her uniform. The smothering mask fit tight but eliminated the powerful stench, so she couldn't complain. She found a set of gloves in the suit's pocket.

Once they were in their garb, they followed Mr. Taylor past workers sorting through boxes of junk. At the far corner of the gigantic room, he set them each at a workstation. A hole to the outside fed a conveyor belt that branched out to individual posts.

She was the last worker Mr. Taylor situated. "When items come down the belt to your station, place them into one of the labeled boxes. Technology, metal, glass, plastic, and organic materials are your options. The most important resources are silicon and precious metals. If you are uncertain whether a metal is of high value, press your hand on the scanner and the computer will attempt to classify the item. If neither you nor the computer can figure it out, press the stop button, and a supervisor will assist."

It sounded simple enough. She nodded.

He reached up and pushed a green button. A robotic voice spoke from the computer. "Reclamation commencing. Hard work lifts us all."

Uncertain if the supervisor monitored her work attitude, she mumbled the response. "Hard work lifts us all."

The reality of her new life hit like catching a twenty-pound weight in the gut. They expected her to stand at this station and process refuse for ten hours a day. *Every day. For the rest of my life. Not good.*

The conveyor belt moved, and the sound of rushing water came from the gaping hole to the outside. Items started down the line, dripping wet, for them to inspect. Just what was on the other side of the wall? Did a machine or a person place items on the conveyor?

I should be grateful I'm not on the side before the cleaning cycle.

Hours dragged by as she sorted broken cell phones, plastic toys, and thousands of plastic bottles. A few books had come through, which she pushed into the organic materials box.

Nana told her about the days when people cut down trees and pulped them into paper to write on. *What a waste.* The Imperium had a way to remove the ink. They converted the paper back into wood pulp to use as garden bedding.

Her back and neck ached from the hard floor, combined with having to reach, pull, and push debris. Thankfully, her work was almost at an end, for today at least. Perhaps her father had been right. She belonged in Administration. A retest might be the best way to go. Back to the drab world of white where at least it was clean and they'd give her a chair.

The belt moving in front of her had a gap between items, which was odd. No, it wasn't a gap, just a necklace. An unusual charm dangled at the end, like a letter *T*. At the intersection of the letter's two arms lay a small red stone. With its yellow-gold color, it could be precious, but who would throw away gold jewelry?

She picked it up and inspected the broken clasp. So perhaps it had fallen into the trash at some point. Uncertain if the metal was real, she laid it back down and pressed the button for the computer to inspect it.

A light scanned across the object, an alarm sounded, and red lights strobed as the computer voice warned. "Contraband detected. Contraband detected. Supervisor alerted."

Pounding feet sounded behind her. Her teammates pivoted to the commotion.

Mr. Taylor's breath came in gasps as he reached her side. "What'd you find?"

Her heart rate had skyrocketed with the noise and confusion. "It's just a necklace. I don't know what the issue is."

He lifted the chain with the strange charm. "Yup. Can't have this floating around. We don't find them all that often, but when we do, they need to be destroyed sooner rather than later. This kind of stuff led to the devastation of our world. Religious nuts fought wars over this junk."

She watched his retreat. Just how could the letter *T* on a necklace cause any problem, much less a war? She'd have to ask Nana tonight.

Exhaustion weighed on her by the time she opened the apartment door at the end of the workday. She was dying to ask Nana about the symbol, but a lively discussion was already in progress.

Mom greeted her with a wrinkled nose as she held her at arm's length instead of her usual hug. "Ooh, sweetie, you need a shower. When you get out, we're helping Nana and Gramps plan what to pack. They've been assigned transport to Solitude tomorrow."

A shock wave rippled through her. "Already?"

Nana's eyes were red and watery. "I'm afraid so. We thought it would be at least a couple of days, but we got the tickets today."

Lexi's world turned upside down.

Chapter 4

Lexi squinted at her watch through burning eyes. Two in the morning. "I can't believe we'll have to say goodbye in a few hours."

Nana zipped her duffle bag shut. "You should try to get a couple of hours' sleep. You've got to work tomorrow. Us old folks can finish sorting through things."

Mom wrapped an arm around Lexi. "Nana's right. You haven't closed your eyes, and you've got a full day tomorrow."

With a roll of her shoulders, Lexi stood and stretched. "At this hour, it isn't like I'm going to fall asleep, anyway. I'd rather power through."

Nana and Gramps's meager possessions shouldn't have taken all evening to pack, but none of them wanted to be apart on this last night together. They would have finished within a few hours if not for the memories they shared as Nana went through a small box of old-fashioned photographs.

Mom rubbed the back of her neck. "I'm going to lie down and close my eyes for an hour."

After Mom left, Nana sat on the couch and patted the seat beside her. "Come on. If you aren't going to sleep, we should sit and relax. We've gotten through everything important."

Lexi plopped down and hugged a pillow to her chest.

Exhaustion weighted her limbs, but her brain couldn't slow down. Wrapped up in the news and then in preparation, she'd almost forgotten about the necklace. "Nana, I found a gold chain with a *T* on it at work yesterday. After the computer scanned it, alarms went off." She tucked her chin into the pillow. "They said it was contraband. Why would the letter *T* be a problem? My supervisor said it caused the disunity that led to the last war. Do you know what that's all about?"

The spark in Nana's eyes said a tale was on its way. How Lexi loved to hear about the before times!

Nana walked to her bag and retrieved her tablet and writing stylus, then drew a replica of the pendant's charm. Her voice dropped to a whisper. "Is this what you saw?"

A chill ran through her. Her tired brain revived with the thrill of secrecy. She dropped her voice low. "Exactly. What's the big deal?"

With a flip, Nana turned the stylus and erased the drawing. "It's called a cross. A group of religious people used to keep it as a relic and a token to show others what they believed."

Nana then drew another icon from two triangles combined into a six-pointed star. "This symbol represented another religion." A third drawing depicted a crescent moon with a star beside it. "And this was another."

The Imperium banned the various creeds after the war. *Unity above all else.* "The beliefs caused the war? The three sides fought?"

With a shake of her head, Nana erased the crescent and star. "It wasn't that simple. There were many religious views—many more. But even *within* each of these three, there were arguments. The ones who used the cross were called Christians. Their groups alone splintered into factions that fought against each other. Even in the country before the Imperium, where it was supposed to be safe to practice your beliefs as you wanted, things got ugly."

"That's why they don't allow religion anymore? It's dangerous?"

Nana's lips thinned into a grim line. "Religion, political groups, differing opinions on values and morals—the Imperium banned anything that caused disagreements. That's why the computers select the Imperium administration according to whom is most qualified. Not by those we liked the best."

What Nana said didn't make sense. "You mean they used to allow people who were popular to run the government?"

"Not exactly, but close." Nana yawned. "I need to catch a little sleep. Why don't we both try?"

How strange the world must have been when religious conviction and popularity contests were still around. The war devastated the land surrounding the few remaining towers that were the Imperium. She'd seen pictures of what lay outside. Even the homeless living in the Favela had it better than any life-form trying to survive out there.

She didn't bother pulling the bed out of the couch. It seemed she'd just laid down when her watch's alarm rumbled on her wrist. With a swipe, she snoozed the noise for five more minutes.

Nana and Mom whispered in the kitchen, but Lexi couldn't make out any of it.

Why was she wasting even five minutes on the couch when this was her last morning with Nana and Gramps? She got up and stretched the ache out of her back. It would have been a smarter idea to take the sixty seconds necessary to pull out her bed last night, instead of sleeping atop the cushions.

The murmuring stopped as Lexi walked into the kitchen and gathered Nana into a hug. "Morning."

After a tight squeeze, Nana pushed Lexi away to look into her eyes, as if drinking in the sight of her, memorizing her features. "Did you sleep well?"

"Well enough." Lexi looked toward her grandparents' bedroom door. "Is Gramps awake?"

Nana's lips flattened. "He's up and moving, but won't be breaking any speed records. Let me go check on him. He wants to spend the morning with you."

After Nana left, Mom caught Lexi in an unexpected embrace. "I don't hug you enough. You know that?"

Lexi couldn't take it if Mom got all mushy this morning. It was all too much. How could she bear never seeing her grandparents again? "I love you too, Mom."

Mom released her, then unclasped her locket from around her neck. "I wanted to give this to you on your birthday, but we didn't have a moment alone." She handed over the necklace. "This was Nana's before it was mine. Now I'm passing it on to you."

The silver chain supported a round charm Lexi had opened many times before. She couldn't resist the urge to unclasp it once again and reveal the photos of her family. One side of the locket displayed a tiny photo of Nana and Gramps. The opposite picture portrayed Mom, Dad, and herself. Mom updated them every few years, so the likenesses were fresh.

"No, it's your favorite piece of jewelry." Lexi closed her fist over it, the metal biting into her palm, digging in and staying, even as she shook her head. "I can't take it from you."

"You can't take something I've already given." Mom stood

tall, as if she'd just completed a mission. "Just like I accepted it from Nana when I turned seventeen."

Mom held her hand out. "Let me put it on you the same way Nana did for me."

Lexi let the silver chain slither into Mom's palm, then turned, and lifted her hair off her neck. "Thanks, Mom."

The pendant lay cool against her throat. Mom tucked it into Lexi's shirt, grasped her shoulders, then spun Lexi back to face her. Her eyes bore into Lexi's, her fingers dug into Lexi's skin, and her deep breath fanned Lexi's face. "This memento has always reminded me of the importance of family. It also reminds me of duty and honor for every generation. Respect for the life we've been given."

Her words must have a deeper meaning. Before Lexi could ask what might lie beneath them, her grandparents' bedroom door opened, and Gramps shuffled out with Nana close behind him. A puff of wind might blow him over, and Nana seemed determined to catch him when it did.

Gramps cleared his throat. "Do I get one of those awesome Lexi hugs before we go?"

Lexi couldn't help her grin as she bounded over, then eased him into her arms. His bony frame had shrunk since the last time she'd squeezed him, and he shook as if it took all his strength to stand. "You can have all the hugs you want this morning, Gramps."

Tears threatened. But she wouldn't let Nana and Gramps's last memories of her be sad, so she bit the inside of her mouth to squelch the emotion.

Mom picked up her recipe book and tucked it under her arm. "Get changed, Lexi. We'll all go down to the tramway together."

Lexi hurried into the bathroom, grabbing a fresh brown uniform on the way. She changed quickly so as not to waste a single moment. After she'd brushed her hair into a ponytail, she gazed at her reflection. Her mother's locket glinted under the garish light. Once again, a tear threatened to form, but she took a deep breath and swiped her eyes.

Dad came into the living area. "Lexi, before you go, we need to talk about your retest."

Heat flashed in her belly. How could he think about that stupid test at a time like this? She didn't want to argue with him now. She wanted the rest of her time with her family to be peaceful. "Can we talk about it tonight, Dad? Nana and Gramps are about ready to go."

His eyes narrowed. "Sure. Tonight."

Mom rejoined the group. Her tablet had replaced the cookbook in her arms. "Well, let's get going. We don't want to miss the transport."

Red and watery, Nana's eyes met Lexi's. She snugged Lexi into a fierce hug that threatened to steal her breath. "I'm going to miss you so much."

The last of Lexi's resolve faltered, and even though she'd bitten her cheek until it bled, the tears came anyway. As she returned Nana's embrace, a sob escaped.

Gramps and Mom merged with them. Arms surrounded Lexi from all directions, and other sniffles combined with hers. A hand caressed the top of her head, and when she looked up, Dad stood beside the group, his right hand on her and his left on her mother's shoulder.

His eyes met hers, and he gave her a nod, his lips in a grim line. "It's getting late. You need to get going. The transports don't wait for laggards."

They gathered the duffle bags and set off. When they reached the air bridge leading to the administrative work building, Dad gave last farewells to his in-laws, kissed Mom goodbye, and pointed at Lexi. "Don't forget. We're talking about the test tonight. I've got it scheduled."

Her curt nod ended the discussion. Dad twisted his lips. He probably wanted to say more. Mentally, she begged him not to argue. Her taut muscles loosened somewhat when he nodded, then left them to head to work.

The rest of them moved on to the elevator bank. As they approached the doors, a purple splash came into view. A light above the camera monitoring the area flashed red. Someone had tagged the elevator doors with the violet, birdlike Y symbol.

Mom hurried to press the button to call the elevator to their floor. "Let's get through before security comes. They'll want to question anyone in the area, and we don't have time."

Lexi glanced at the camera. Someone had painted the lens over just like when they'd tagged the symbol on the air bridge. "What's it all about, Mom? What does someone hope to gain by defacing public property? They'll end up in jail—or worse."

The doors slid open, and Mom rushed them in. "There are those who don't agree with the government's decisions. They want to change the world."

Gramps leaned on the handrail. His hands shook. "Maybe they've got the right idea."

"Dad." Mom's whisper was barely audible. She glared. "Not here."

At the transport level, the time had come. Lexi would have to turn left to catch her tram to work. Nana and Gramps would head right toward the transport to Solitude.

Lexi's determination not to cry had weakened, and a lump clogged her throat. With a plastered-on smile, she gave both of her grandparents last kisses on their cheeks. "I love you."

When she backed away from them, Mom surprised her with a crushing embrace. "I'm going to walk them to their transport. You get to work so you're not late. I love you."

Lexi pulled back. Mom's eyes weren't dry, either. "I love you too. I'll see you tonight."

Mom's damp eyes hardened with something indecipherable. Before Lexi could ask, Mom twirled away and herded Nana and Gramps toward the opposite end of the transportation building.

A peek at her watch told Lexi she needed to hurry to avoid a demerit. She trotted in for the tram to the other buildings.

Loneliness overwhelmed her as she stood in line. Though they'd expressed their love for each other and embraced multiple times, it no longer satisfied the void. If only she could skip work today and spend a few more moments with them.

A shout echoed from the direction her family had gone. She turned as an orange ball of flame filled the loading zone on the far end. A microsecond later, an explosion rocked the entire area. The blast catapulted her into the air.

Chapter 5

White-hot pain ripped through Lexi's skull while shards of color danced behind her closed eyelids. She had to break free from this dark misery. With a concentrated effort, she slit her eyelids open, then slammed them shut to escape the blinding brightness.

"Lexi. Wake up, baby girl." Her father's voice, combined with the warmth of his firm hand on hers, was a command. "I need you to open your eyes."

She lifted her arm to fend off the blaze as she squinted, but tubes running out of the back of her hand tugged it down. Then she remembered, and her eyelids flew open despite the pain, fluttering in the glare. "There was an explosion. Where's Mom? Nana... Gramps?"

When her gaze found her father's, wrinkles she'd never seen before framed his red eyes. A white streak ran through his hair. His Adam's apple bobbed as he squeezed her hand. "They're... " His voice broke, and he swallowed a sob. A tear slipped down one cheek. "They're gone, baby girl. Mom, Nana, and Gramps—everyone in the transport to Solitude is dead or missing."

She wrenched her hand out of his. What was this "baby girl" stuff, anyway? Her father had never been the mushy type. She closed her eyes. He must be confused. With his years working security within the Administration building, he'd have known if something bad was going to happen. "No. They weren't that far from me. Right on the other side of the tunnel. I'm okay. They should be too."

His head fell to his chest, and a sob escaped. "They aren't here, baby girl. I'm sorry."

The crush of his hand reclaiming hers was an anvil, determined to drag her under the wave of sorrow he couldn't free them from. She resisted at first, then realized—Mom would be here in the medical unit if she were alive. Nana too. They'd never leave her father to sit with her if they could avoid it. The sorrow pulled her under, and she struggled to breathe.

By the end of the day, they released Lexi with orders for her father to monitor her for complications. Her head pounded like a tiny army had set to war in her skull. Her vision swam with every step, so the haggard-faced nurse put her into a wheelchair to get home.

Lexi couldn't wait to get out of the unit. During the night, staff whispered about the bombing when they thought she was asleep. The Imperium claimed the explosion came from a faulty generator, but the word *rebel* came up in murmured hallway conversations. Could Y have transitioned from spray-painting graffiti to sabotage? They were the only group she knew of.

Her father opened their apartment door. A deafening silence greeted them, and she wanted to cry.

No. Not cry. She wanted to scream. A terrorist act, if the rumors were true, had taken everything from her. She wanted to find Y—to hold someone accountable.

After Father parked her chair beside the table, he got a protein bar out of the kitchen, filled a glass with water, and placed them both in front of her. "You should eat something. Keep up your strength."

She stared at the yellow wrapper with red lettering. Scientists designed the colors to stimulate the part of the brain that drove the need to eat. She'd learned that, along with so many useless bits of information, to prepare for work in Administration. What did it matter now?

Father returned to the table and plopped a worker tablet down in front of her. "This came for you today. I'm certain it has your new apartment assignment in it, but we're both granted a week of mourning."

She clamped her teeth on her tongue to keep from spitting her thoughts out. When she transitioned away from a student tablet to a worker tablet, she'd hoped it would have information on running the greenhouses. Her dream shriveled smaller in her heart at the sight of it.

The government would have linked the new device to the communication systems of her assigned job. It wouldn't be only an apartment. A mate would go along with that new address. Next would come health department appointments where they'd probe and prod every month until the first child arrived.

A new couple's highest priority was to make a baby, to expand the Imperium's youthful population.

A shudder shook her from head to toe. How could anyone expect her to marry a stranger and turn into some sort of baby factory?

Thoughts of the rebellion sounded pretty good. She'd stage her own revolt and refuse to open her tablet or read the notification waiting for her. They'd have to drag her, kicking and screaming up a storm, to whatever address they'd assigned.

But her father still hovered beside the table as if lost in thought. His eyes were unfocused, the lines on his face deeper than when she'd first woken in the healthcare unit. How could she have been so selfish not to realize his world had just ended? She wasn't the only one suffering.

Pushing aside the anger, the thoughts of her grandparents and her mother, she allowed grief in once again. "Father..."

His gaze darted to hers, and he moved to her faster than she'd thought him capable. "What do you need?"

The pain in his eyes seemed to eclipse her own. As she stood, her legs quaked, and her head spun. He understood and caught her into a hug.

Together, they cried for all they'd lost.

A jolt woke Lexi in an instant. With a shake of her wrist, she realized she'd overslept her work alarm, which triggered the heavy-handed tactic to rouse her. With a swipe, she deactivated it, then forced herself to sit on the edge of her bed.

The silence in the kitchen, normally filled with Mom and Nana's whispered conversations, seemed amplified.

Her father came out of the bathroom, his wet hair slicked back, and his administrative whites pressed and starched. "Morning. I've been called into an emergency meeting. I need to take care of a few things after that." He ran a hand down his arm as if to smooth out a nonexistent wrinkle. "How are you feeling?"

Figures. She'd wondered how he'd handle an entire week of staying away from his precious administrative role. Now she knew. *He wouldn't.* "Fine."

He moved into the kitchen and grabbed a bar out of the cupboard. "We need to talk, Lexi."

So true. But he wouldn't want to discuss the same things she did. "Can it wait?"

A breath of air whooshed out of his mouth, and he closed his eyes. She knew the look, his what-am-I-going-to-do-with-you look. "No. It can't."

She didn't want to fight. Not now. "I'm listening."

He sat at the table, then waved her over.

Compliant as an automaton, she took the seat opposite.

"Lexi, I've got your retest scheduled. If you score high enough, you'll be back in school for another two years. I know you can get a better job. The Imperium needs engineers."

She stared at her hands on the table. Heading back to the classroom appealed to a tiny part of her. A return to the familiar and the ability to put off the role of wife and mother would be a relief. If she went along, though, she'd give up any chance of leaving the white world she'd been in for the last seventeen years. She'd die here. Her father would never understand. "I can't."

He grasped her hand. "Look at me."

When she raised her head, sadness wasn't what sheened his eyes. Worry, perhaps even panic, had his pupils dilated. The look set her heart thumping. "What's wrong?"

His hand squeezed hers. "When you move out, I have to leave too. They reserve apartments for people with children to raise." He rubbed the back of her hand with his thumb. "If you stay in school, I've got two more years before I have to move to the dorms. Wouldn't you like two more years?"

So that was it. He wasn't worried about her or sad about

losing Mom. He was stressed about being forced into the men's dorms.

She yanked her hand out of his grasp. "You'd better get to work. You don't want to be late for your precious meeting."

He lurched back as if she'd slapped him. His face reddened, and his eyes hardened. "We'll talk again tonight."

It took an hour alone in the apartment, lying on her mattress, before her heart rate returned to normal. Her stomach ached with either hunger or anxiety. The thought of a nutrition bar nauseated her, so food was out.

She wandered into her grandparents' bedroom. The neatly made bed, topped with Nana's hand-stitched pillowcases, looked abandoned. Two small boxes sat in the corner—all that she had left of them. Her hand reached for the locket Mom had given her, her sole remaining connection with Nana, Gramps, and Mom.

No. There was something else.

She shuffled to her parents' room. The bruises and aches left from the explosion prevented anything faster than a solid plod. Inside, she breathed in deeply, letting the spartan white room her parents had shared envelop her.

She moved to the closet, her mother's clothes on the right side, her father's on the left. A shelf overhead held small boxes. It must be there. She opened each one until she found what she'd been searching for—the cookbook.

Hugging it to her chest, she let the tears flow until she crumpled to the floor, sobbing, and clutching the one other artifact Mom had touched every day.

By the time the tears ran out, she wasn't certain how long she'd sat there. She took the book back to the kitchen table.

What was so special about this antique book? The archives

were available on her tablet if Mom wanted a recipe for some exotic meal. It wasn't like they had fresh food regularly. Mom said she loved to create new dishes, but could a dream of being able to cook proper food keep her poring over recipes every morning?

Lexi needed to understand. Perhaps the answer to being close to her mother was between the cardboard covers. She inspected the first page. It started with an introduction from the author. Next came tips for the home cook, then a table of contents for the various recipe groups.

The photos made her hungry. Maybe that was what had her mother so enamored with the tome—seeing all the beautiful food when her world was mostly bland nutrition bars. Like a wish book.

She continued flipping through the pages, pausing at photos, ingredient lists, and instructions for creating sumptuous dishes to please the palate.

About a quarter of the way through, she flipped the page, and a shiver shot down her spine. The book had a hole in it. Someone had cut a square through the remaining pages to create a hiding place. And the hole wasn't empty. Nestled inside rested another book. A violet hardback cover with curving letters that spelled out the words *My Diary*.

It wasn't about the recipes, after all. No wonder Mom never left it out for others to pick up. It held her most precious thoughts. Now Lexi had them.

She tipped the larger book over and let the diary drop to the table while protecting the cookbook pages. Mom had kept it pristine and safe for as long as Lexi could remember. Lexi would as well.

With reverence, she lifted the purple book's front flap, eager to know her mother's most intimate secrets, longing to be close to her once more. A twinge struck. Was this an intrusion? No. Mom couldn't hurt anymore. It could only help now.

Still, Lexi wasn't prepared for the design on the first page—a neat drawing of a violet stylized Y. The rebel symbol. Her heart raced and stole her breath away. Could Mom have been a part of the movement fighting against the Imperium? Impossible. If she had been, she'd still be alive and not blown into unrecoverable pieces by the rebel's bomb. Had she dabbled in the group and turned against them? If so, had she been a target?

This tome went beyond contraband. This could get her and her father locked up permanently—or worse.

Her fingers shook and clumsily turned the page to the first entry. It dated back to the days right after Lexi's birth.

> I'm holding my baby in my arms for the first time. It's like a surgeon removed a piece of my heart and placed it into this tiny body. I keep counting her miniature fingers and toes, just to be sure, but she's perfect. Though I hated the thought of being forced to have a baby, now that Lexi is here, I can't imagine my world without her.
>
> Gunner smiles all the time, though he avoids holding Lexi. Obviously, he's thrilled we're being assigned a larger apartment, one with two bedrooms. That second room will be vacant for a while, though. I can't imagine letting her out of my sight anytime soon. He's already mentioned trying for a boy next. I worry he only cares about the rewards the Imperium hands out. Why doesn't he hold her?
>
> I want to give my girl everything I couldn't have. She

should be allowed to choose her career... her husband.
To marry for love instead of to further the cause of the
Imperium.

But how can I make that happen? She should have
what I couldn't.

She'd known her mother wasn't the solid supporter of the
Imperium her father was. Not that Mom would ever have said
the words out loud. But did this prove she'd taken her lack of
faith in the Imperium to the next level? Had she supported the
rebellion in spirit, or was she actively involved? The simple
act of owning a book that contained the rebel symbol would
be enough for the Freedom Force to arrest her, but had there
been more?

A chime sounded, and Lexi slammed the book shut. Someone was at the door. Was it possible the Imperium had cameras
in the apartment? Could they know she had the diary and what
it contained?

The sound came again. She slid the diary back into the
cookbook, then closed the cover to protect it from straying
eyes.

She tucked the book safely inside a drawer, then activated
the camera view from the hallway outside. Courtney. What
was her nosy next-door neighbor doing home at this hour?

Lexi opened the door to Courtney holding a thermos in one
hand and a single daisy in the other.

Courtney's face broke into a smile. "Oh, I'm so glad you're
well enough to be up and out of bed. I was so worried when
I saw you come past our door in a wheelchair." She stepped
into the room, uninvited. "Dad gave me a few credits when
we heard about your mom and grandparents. I brought you

47

some bullion and this flower. It was expensive, but since we're neighbors and all, I figured you'd appreciate the support."

Lexi's hands balled into fists at her sides, and she bit the inside of her lip. She'd known Courtney long enough to know support was the last thing on her neighbor's mind. What she wanted was the inside scoop. Something to gossip about to garner the attention she craved. Last year, she'd carried on for weeks with the news an older classmate had run off before graduation to avoid being mated.

Lexi wanted to return to her mother's diary, not deal with a glory seeker. But she had to be cautious. Courtney and her family loved the Imperium and any opportunity to point out anyone who wasn't 100 percent loyal. "Thank you so much for thinking of me. I'll put that in water right away." She reached out, but Courtney didn't hand the thermos and flower over. Lexi pressed. "As you can imagine, I'm not feeling my best right now. I'm certain you understand."

Courtney's gaze roamed the apartment as if looking for anything out of place. Then she relinquished the gifts. "Of course. I'll let you rest. We'll talk more later, okay?"

Lexi held both items in one hand while she opened the door with the other. "For sure. Later."

She closed the door the moment Courtney was beyond the threshold. No way would she be talking to her neighbor about what she'd found. That was her secret to hold. Not even her father would hear the story from Lexi.

Chapter 6

For what had to have been the tenth time in the last hour, Lexi checked her watch, afraid she'd lose track of time. Time flew by when she was reading Mom's diary. Though Mom wrote mostly about her new baby and how tired she was, Lexi drank in every word, desperate to be close.

If she hurried, she had enough time to find something special for dinner before her father came home. While she wasn't a fan of his Lexi-must-be-an-engineer plan, she didn't want to argue either. Like it or not, he was the only family she had left. The thought burrowed a hole in her chest. Why did their relationship have to be so challenging?

A tear slipped down her cheek. She'd never been so alone in the world. The first person she'd have gone to with her hurts would have been Nana. Lexi couldn't help but smile at the memory of coming home from school, fresh from an argument with Aponi. Nana had wrapped Lexi in her arms and told her a story about the before times. Those tales always took Lexi's mind off her problems.

But she'd never hear another story from Nana. Never feel Gramps's warm embrace. Never receive a knowing wink from Mom when Lexi aced a test. Looking around the apartment, the emptiness was too much. Perhaps it would be good to get into the new apartment. To get away from the memories and the loss.

Enough whining. Sitting around by herself only amplified the problem. She headed down the hallway toward the elevator. The aches and pains hadn't let up, but the dizziness had passed. For that, she was grateful.

While she waited at the elevator bank, she glanced at the security cameras. No wonder Mom kept the book hidden. The first page was incriminating enough. Surely, Dad didn't know about the diary and what it contained. With his job in security, he'd often complained about how foolish people were to go against the Imperium. If he found the journal, he'd destroy it.

Who knew what she'd find as she dug deeper into her mother's private thoughts. The diary might reveal secrets that put both Lexi and her father in danger. Was she an idiot to hang onto it?

Destroying it would protect not only her mother's reputation but also her father's job and safety. If she let it go, she'd never know the truth, though. She couldn't give up the chance to learn more about Mom. The risk was worth it.

The elevator doors opened and beckoned her in. After the brief ride upward, the elevator released her into a world she'd dreamed of working in for years. This should have been her assignment. Not Reclamation. Sunlight greeted her through the clear walls that separated the elevator queuing area from the greenhouse, and she let the frustration go.

The moment she walked through the glass doors, moist heat enveloped her. The scents of water, earth, and flowering plants calmed and centered her. Why couldn't the Imperium have trained her to work here instead of engineering?

A pool of reddish-brown water bubbled beside a path through the hydroponic growing tubes. She'd learned enough from her research to know the liquid's color came from nutrients the gardeners put into it to feed the plants.

A trickle of fluids moved through pumps and tubes. She'd arrived in time to watch one of the day's five plant feedings. She walked along the path to the salesroom. Being stuck in slow-motion mode didn't bother her when she wandered through the greenhouse. The sun warmed her skin, and she tipped her face upward to drink more in.

Reaching up, she ran her fingertips over tender spinach leaves. Salad was one of her favorites when they treated themselves to fresh food. Most of the high-protein greens would end up in nutrition bars or on the plates of those much higher in rank than her family. Strange how those in the top administrative positions received better food than the rest of the Imperium. With great minds came great privilege. Or at least that's what her father always said.

She flicked her wrist to check her watch. He'd be home soon. No time to dawdle. Near the path's far end, a door led into the store's cooler environment. The store had air-conditioning, along with solid walls and roof. Peas, spinach, and green beans were available for purchase by those who had special occasions to celebrate—and enough credits to afford the luxury.

A sweet aroma drew her to a display lined with baskets of freshly picked strawberries. Perfect. She hovered over the display and basked in the delicate perfume. While she loved the berries, they weren't her favorite compared with some of the other treats available. This splurge wasn't about her, though. It was about her father. These red fruits rose to the top of his preferences list.

Tonight, she'd treat him to his favorite dessert. Perhaps that would put him in a better mood and ease the discussion about her retaking the placement test. Or her refusal.

Before opening their apartment door, Lexi wanted nothing more than to sit and rest. Every inch of her ached. She let her eyes slip shut for a brief respite, but she forced them open when she saw the explosion again in her mind. *Nope. Not going there.*

Father had arrived home before her and waited in the kitchen, chewing on a protein bar. His lips slanted downward, hinting his workday had been difficult—or he expected his evening would be. She hoped for the former, but feared the latter more accurate.

She set the strawberries on the counter. "I picked up a peace offering. I don't want to fight."

He nodded, wadded the empty wrapper, and tossed it in the recycle bin. "I guess that answers my question then. Why won't you follow through with the retest?"

The disappointment dulling his eyes brought back memories of his scolding any time she failed to ace an exam. Years' worth of you-can-do-better lectures. But the look had the opposite effect this time. She was an adult now. He could glare all he wanted to, but it only solidified her decision. "I can't. I need to follow my own path. The life in engineering, in Administration, isn't for me."

He crossed his arms, and his gaze hardened. "You'd rather pick through garbage for the rest of your life than use your brain? Few people have the mental discipline to be an engineer. You're wasting your intellect."

Tension stiffened her shoulders. They'd had this argument so many times. With the connections he had, she'd begged him to call in favors. He could've gotten her into the greenhouse. Instead, he'd said it was beneath her. Now he'd have to live with her corresponding choice. "I'm happy to be anywhere outside of Administration, especially engineering."

His lips pursed as if he'd finalized a decision. When his stare returned to hers, the determination in his eyes warned she might have pushed him too far, one too many times. "Then I have no other choice. I didn't want to have to do this, but if you're resolved not to take the test again, I need to take care of myself."

His words sounded ominous. What could he be up to?

"I guess we both need to do what we need to."

Standing straight, he put his hands in his pockets. "You know they'll reassign me to the dorms the moment you move out. Apartments are for families with children or those who are trying for a child. My only other option is to take a new wife." He paused and set his jaw. "I'm requesting an assignment."

The world froze in place, and ice filled her belly. She couldn't have heard correctly. Sure, her parents had their differences, but they'd been together for eighteen years. Now would be the time to offer for him to live with her and her new husband, but he didn't deserve any grace. He'd gone too far. "No. You... you can't just replace Mom like she didn't matter."

His eyes widened, and his hands came out pleading. "Don't you get it? I *won't* live in the dorms now that I have an option to remarry. Once I move there, my career is over. Instead, I can have a fresh start. You could have a brother or sister. Wouldn't that be great?"

The cynical laugh that tumbled out of her mouth said he didn't deserve kindness. "Well then, I guess congratulations are due, aren't they? I hope you'll both be very happy."

With a swipe of her arm, she sent the strawberry container flying off the counter. Turning her back on him, she stormed into her grandparents' bedroom and claimed the privacy. After pacing around the bed and back for what seemed an eternity, she calmed her heart.

What was he doing? How could he bring another woman in to replace Mom as if she'd been a possession he'd misplaced? *It's not our home anymore. It's his. I've got a new home waiting for me in Reclamation.*

She had no fuel left to stoke the flames in her heart, and the fire burned out, leaving coals aglow with hurt in its place. She dropped onto the bed and hugged Nana's pillow close, ready to release the pent-up pain. Tears flowed until she had nothing left but hiccups and a soggy pillow cover.

All she wanted was to have her family back. Mom, Nana, and Gramps. They'd understand what her father never could. He didn't love *her*, only the prestige that having an engineer for a daughter could provide. She'd denied him that, so he had no need for her. She was alone in the world.

Lexi waited hours before she assumed her father had gone to bed. To be certain, she cracked open the bedroom door and peeked out—no sign of him. She made her way into the kitchen and slid the cookbook from its hiding place.

The book and its hidden secrets were hers now. She'd never let him have it. Now that she knew how little her mother meant to him, she knew Mom never would have told him anything about her disagreements with the Imperium.

She closed the bedroom door on him and locked it. Using a pillow to prop herself against the headboard, she opened the cookbook and dumped out the diary. She needed to know how far her mother had taken her lack of faith in the Imperium.

The next entry pulled her into Mom's past again.

Lexi is so precious and such a wonderful baby. She's already sleeping all night. What a lucky mother I am. Even though she's easy to care for, I'm still exhausted. Mom says it'll take a while for me to get my strength back since it was such a difficult birth.

Gunner doesn't understand. He expects me to snap back and be ready to try for a brother or sister to Lexi. If it's up to him, we'll have ten children, enough to get the largest apartment the Imperium permits. After such a difficult pregnancy and delivery, the thought of trying again right away scares me.

Mom had never said much about Lexi's birth, much less mentioned there were complications. If only Mom could be with her now. So many questions begged to be asked. Why hadn't she taken the time to talk to Mom more when they'd been together? Lexi wanted to scream at her younger self for being so self-centered. Mom, Nana, and Gramps had been there every day. If she'd asked, they'd have told her so many more stories. Perhaps Mom would have even told the truth about the rebels and what her involvement was—or wasn't.

Lexi flipped the page.

Back from the doctor's office. The news isn't good. I'm not sure how to tell Gunner there won't be any more children. We're lucky to have our little Lexi, but I doubt he'll see it that way. He's going to be angry for sure.

Bile burned in Lexi's stomach. If only she could go back in

time and hug her mom right after she'd written those words. How awful to be afraid to tell your husband you couldn't have another child. Her parents had often been cool toward each other. Had it all started with the day Mom found out Lexi would be their only child? Her father's plan to improve his status wouldn't happen.

The next entry made her grind her teeth.

Gunner was furious. He wants me to get a second opinion, as if a different doctor could change my body.

I told him we need to be content with the gift we have in Lexi, but of course, Gunner is who he is. It's not enough.

How can my heart be breaking at the same time as Lexi's tiny fingers wrap around my thumb? I knew my marriage wouldn't be full of love at first, but I'd hoped after the baby arrived Gunner would settle down and get past his need to impress everyone and advance his career. Instead, it's made him even more determined to prove he's committed to the Imperium and all it stands for.

A round deformity marred the page in the center of the entry. The ink had smeared. It didn't take the brain of an engineer to realize a drop of moisture had created the circle. Lexi ran her finger over the smudge—her mother's tear.

Her throat swelled as her eyes filled and the words on the page blurred. The temptation to storm out of the bedroom and demand an apology from her father for the pain he'd inflicted overwhelmed her.

It wasn't as if he'd changed much over the years. He simply had a new target for his anger—Lexi.

The headache from her concussion returned. She had a few

short days to mourn before the Imperium expected her to be back to work. Worse than that. They expected her to marry some strange half-wit who would most likely be as bad as her father.

She slipped the diary into the safety of the cookbook and tucked it in between the mattress and the bed frame. There would be plenty of time to read the rest of Mom's entries. Perhaps there would be happier thoughts as the years went by. After all, her mother hadn't seemed depressed or even sad. Somehow, Mom had moved past her hurt or channeled it somewhere.

A knock jarred Lexi. Having no desire to speak to her father, she didn't respond.

His voice, normally authoritative, sounded almost pleading. "Lexi, can we talk?"

No.

The doorknob turned, then jiggled once he realized she'd locked it. That should tell him everything he needed to know about how she felt about him right now.

She rolled onto the bed, pulled her grandparents' pillows into a hug, and breathed in the scent of them. Nana's smelled like the special perfume they'd all saved up to buy for her birthday every year. Gramps's smelled less pleasant, more like illness. Nevertheless, it was him. With deep inhalations, she closed her eyes and thought of them.

If they were still alive, she'd be with Mom and Nana right now, whispering about Lexi's new mate and what he'd be like. Gramps would tease them and say they were a bunch of cackling hens. She'd give anything to be the target of Gramps's ribbing one more time.

She thought back to her first day on the job and Ethan.

Would her assigned husband be anything like him? A girl could dream.

Chapter 7

Everything hurt. Lexi had ignored her father's knock earlier in the morning and enjoyed another hour of sleep before forcing herself to face the day. Her injuries from the explosion amplified overnight and left her stiff and sore. Only one solution for that—get up.

Once she'd planted both feet on the floor, she stretched her limbs and back. She wouldn't waste her time off from Reclamation. With the new day, she needed to accept the life she'd chosen.

Time to check out her apartment. No way did she want to have to live with her father and his replacement wife. A shudder ran through her.

She padded out to the kitchen, picked up her tablet, and pulled up the messages. There were three.

> *Congratulations on your graduation and assignment to the Reclamation towers. Your new apartment number is 1047. You may transfer any personal belongings as we have set your security clearance.*

That was that. She officially had a home of her own. Well, almost her own. The second message informed her of her new roommate.

> *Congratulations on your upcoming nuptials. Based on the Imperium's advanced genetic mapping results and aptitude profiles, as well as personality strengths and weaknesses, your perfect match is Reeves Scheffer.*

The message informed her the wedding was tomorrow, which stole her breath away. Her hands shook by the time she'd garnered the courage to open the third message.

> *The Imperium administrative team wishes to express our deepest condolences for the loss of your mother and grandparents. Because of the mourning period, the date of your wedding has been rescheduled.*

The new date gave her five days to deal with her loss. That was all the Imperium allotted her for grief. Then they expected her to show up, ready to start married life with her "perfect" match. As if she could put a timer on her broken heart, it'd automatically mend, and she'd be ready to celebrate after an arbitrary amount of time. Ludicrous.

She did the math. Today was already the third mourning day. Two more days of freedom before she became Mrs. Scheffer. *Shoot.* She had to change her name. That stunk. Maybe Reeves would be willing to use her last name instead. The Imperium permitted it *if* both agreed. Though Mrs. Verity would soon be her new stepmom's name. *Nope. Not doing that.*

Reeves. What were the chances he'd be good-looking or even friendly like Ethan on her first day at Reclamation?

Visions of Aponi sprang into focus as she thought of marriage. Her best friend's excitement at getting hitched to her dream guy had nauseated Lexi for the past year. Had Aponi already been through the ceremony? If so, was she happy with her assigned husband?

Lexi opened the tablet's messaging system, found Aponi still listed under her maiden name, and sent her a note. She'd better connect to the one person in her life she *didn't* hate right now.

She wouldn't waste another minute worrying about whom the powers above had matched her. That was a problem for two days from today. At this moment, she wanted to get out of this apartment before her father brought the new Mrs. Verity home.

Her aching muscles wished for hotter water while she showered. The more she moved, the more flexibility returned to her body, so by the time she'd dressed in her brown uniform and packed her few belongings, she felt almost human again.

She opened Mom's locket before she put it on, wanting to see the faces she missed smile back at her. What she wouldn't give to have one more hug. *Huh.* Her grandparents' picture sat crooked in the frame. How had that happened?

There had to be a way to straighten it, so she fiddled with the charm, searching for the seam to open the tiny frame. But wait. She could twist the entire picture. She jiggled, and in doing so, it slid off completely.

Her breath caught in her throat. Behind the photo sat the stylized Y icon. What in the Imperium? It had to be some sort of identification. Why else would Mom hide a symbol on her body that could get her thrown into prison or worse? Had Mom forgotten it was there before she'd given the necklace to her?

And the piece originated with Nana. There had to be more

to that fact. Had her grandmother been part of the rebellion? It was almost too much to process. What if she hadn't truly known either Nana or Mom? Now it was too late.

That didn't mean she couldn't learn more, though. But first, she needed to get out of this place.

She stashed the photo back as soon as she could make her shaking hands cooperate. Once it was straight, she fastened it back around her neck. She wedged the cookbook underneath the clothes in her backpack, then placed her tablet on top, zipped it closed, and flung it across her shoulder. Time to check out her new home.

At the transportation platform, debris-filled dumpsters cordoned off the loading area for Solitude. Black soot covered most surfaces. Workers stood on scaffolding, busy reinforcing the tunnel's walls and ceiling, while temporary steel beams held up the remaining roof.

A cane poked out from under a sizeable chunk of cement. She shuddered, her chest constricting so tight she fought to breathe. Someone's grandparent had been holding it when the blast went off. One news report said the force and temperature of the explosion had obliterated many of the bodies.

Two men in white hard hats and Administration uniforms jabbed at their tablets and pointed to various areas of destruction. If she'd completed her engineering program, she'd be one of those who planned rebuilds like the one they managed now.

Nausea rose in her throat with the acrid assault on her nose. She hurried to catch the next tram, fleeing the memory of the catastrophe, the flames still too alive in her mind.

The tram ride to the Brown building ended before she could clear the gruesome vibes. Grateful for the task, she followed the signs to the apartment tower and rode the elevator to the tenth floor.

She hesitated at her apartment door. What if Reeves was in there? Should she knock? No. This was *her* home now. She placed her palm on the scanner. It flared green, and the lock clicked free.

After a deep, cleansing breath, she turned the knob and entered.

The apartment had the same efficient arrangement as the one she'd lived in for as long as she could remember. The lack of a second bedroom door seemed to be the only difference. They wouldn't qualify for a two-bedroom apartment until a baby arrived.

A shade the color of dead moss covered the walls, as if she'd forget which building she was in if the walls weren't brown.

Until this moment, she'd not thought much about the fact that everyone had the same table, the same couch, and the same counters. The Imperium valued uniformity, but this took the concept to the extreme.

A quick wander through the rooms confirmed the place held everything they needed except for personal items. She should've brought some shampoo and soap. She'd have credits from work deposited into her Imperium account, but it wouldn't be much since she'd worked only one day before the explosion.

She dropped her backpack on the couch and flopped down beside it. Now what?

The click of the door lock releasing drew her attention, and she sprang up at the same time as the door swung open. A young guy, who had to be Reeves, stepped in, a backpack hanging off one shoulder.

He had to be at least six feet tall with a strong nose and blond bangs framing blue eyes. They connected with her own, and he grinned. "Honey, I'm home."

Her heart raced at being in the same room with him. What do you say to someone you've never even met but you're expected to sleep with in a few short days? Should she shake his hand? Did he expect a hug? Would he kiss her?

Eeps. Why are you thinking about kissing? This is wrong on so many levels. Unable to think what to do with her hands, she jammed them into her jumpsuit pockets. "Funny."

The backpack slid off his shoulder, and he tossed it beside hers. His grin morphed into a smirk. "We're stuck in this together. We might as well make the best of an awkward situation."

Tension wound around her limbs to the point where she ached to run, if only for the outlet exercise would provide. "We shouldn't even be in this situation. The Imperium shouldn't have the right to tell me whom to marry or even *if* I marry, for that matter. What if I want to be alone for the rest of my life?"

Shoot. Way to throw your thoughts out there, Lexi. What if he reported her for seditious behavior?

He sucked his lips in as if struggling not to smile, fueling her anger to the point it overcame her concerns. Then he shrugged. "What if the Imperium is right? What if humans can't make the most important decisions on their own? You know the history as well as I do. Before the war, people got divorced all the time, right? Families fell apart. Childhood depression reached epic proportions." He strolled to the couch and flopped to join the backpacks. The way he crossed his legs at the ankles and his hands behind his head made him look like he didn't have a care in the world. "The childbirth rates dropped into the basement when people made their own choices. At least this way, we know our DNA will make strong, healthy babies."

As if she wanted to make a baby with him. "I think you tested wrong. You shouldn't be working in Reclamation. You should be writing slogans for the Imperium."

He rolled his gorgeous eyes. "Aw, come on. Lighten up."

Good thing her father didn't know she'd stormed out of the house. The Imperium had given her time for mourning. She'd be stupid not to take every minute they allotted. "I'm not staying anyway, not tonight."

"I heard about your mom and grandparents." His smile vanished, and his eyes softened. "I'm so sorry. Of course, you need time to grieve. Anything that I can do, just let me know."

Figures. He seemed to be a nice guy and had more muscles on his arms than she'd thought possible. What would it feel like to have them wrapped around her?

No! Not going there. He's not your choice. He's the Imperium's.

She wasn't some automaton they'd programmed to do their bidding. No matter how good-looking he was.

The more time she spent in the room with him, the more her heart ached to let him into it and accept his comfort. Someone must have sucked all the oxygen out of the room. She couldn't seem to get enough air. Nice guy or not, she had to get away. "I gotta go. Just wanted to see the place for myself. Shouldn't you be at work?"

She grabbed for her backpack, but he got there a second ahead of her.

He picked it up, stood, and held the straps out as if to help her put it on. "I had to work a double last night, so got today off. I'd hoped I might find you here. I look forward to getting to know you better, Lexi."

No way would she allow him to put it over her shoulders. She snagged one strap and hugged the bag into her chest. "Sure."

She couldn't get to the front door fast enough. His footsteps followed her, and panic tightened her chest, squeezing the remaining air out of her lungs. What if he tried to keep her from leaving?

He beat her to the door, but instead of blocking her, he opened it. "Take care. We'll talk again soon."

Her heart rate didn't slow until the door clicked behind her. She looked back on an empty hallway—not following her. Whew. What a relief.

Where should she go? Her father wouldn't care if she returned to their apartment. No, she couldn't deal with him right now. She needed Mom or Nana or even Gramps. Anyone but Dad.

How about her best friend? She pulled out the tablet and looked up Aponi's address in the Administration building.

Lexi sent a quick message asking to meet up and started back to the transportation area. Before she got to the tram, a return message invited her over to see Aponi's new home and said how sorry she was about Lexi's loss. She couldn't handle seeing a frown on her BFF's face. Right now, she needed the bright sunny butterfly Aponi's mother had named her after. In her reply, she told her friend she wanted to focus on the future, not on what was gone.

She had the tram to herself, mostly. Near the end of the same car, a mother wore the white uniform of Administration and held a young girl on her lap. The little one had ringlets of golden hair framing her cherubic cheeks. The two snuggled close while the mom whispered something into the girl's ear that evoked a toothy grin. Thoughts of Lexi's mother brought an ache she couldn't rub away. A tear slipped out, and she scrubbed it away with her sleeve.

The tram stopped at the White building, and Lexi exited. Eagerness to be with Aponi—to feel the warmth of affection only a friend could provide—overwhelmed her.

She rode the elevator to the building's fourth floor and wandered down the hall until she reached the apartment number Aponi had given her. Her two quick raps on the door echoed down the empty hallway. A camera moved above the door, so Lexi waved at it. *Come on, Aponi. Be home.*

The lock disengaging brought hope. The door opened, and Aponi's smile seemed wide enough to fill the doorway on its own. A shrill squeal emanated from her as she torpedoed into Lexi's arms. "Come in! Welcome to our new home."

Lexi struggled to extricate herself from Aponi's death grip while her friend bounced. "Hey, good to see you too, but you're choking me. Let me live long enough to see your place."

Aponi released Lexi, then sprang back into the apartment, arms wide as she twirled in a circle. "This is it. Our love nest." Once Lexi stepped inside, Aponi dashed behind her and closed the door. "Trev isn't home right now. He had some paperwork to take care of. We're on our honeymoon. Can you *believe* it?"

Aponi drew a heart on her chest with her finger, then *giggled*... like a little kid.

Lexi might vomit. How was it possible that someone who still giggled could be married? "You seem happy."

Aponi's eyebrows rose, and her eyes grew wide. She clasped her hands in front of her chest and grinned like a fool. "Happy? I'm ecstatic. Wait till you meet Trev. He's so cute. I'm a lucky girl."

Her friend couldn't understand how disturbing seeing her dumbstruck with love was. For as long as Lexi could remember, Aponi had been infatuated with the idea of love. Lexi couldn't bring Aponi down now. Not when bliss oozed from her every pore. It wouldn't be right.

Life would be so much easier if she could just accept the reality of the Imperium assigning her to a mate. If only she could be like her friend. But that wasn't how Mom had raised Lexi. This life wouldn't do for her. She wanted out.

Chapter 8

Lexi inspected her image in the bathroom mirror. Had it only been three days since the explosion? A bruise on her cheek faded to green. Only two days of freedom remained before the Imperium expected her to marry Reeves. Three honeymoon days later, Reclamation would demand her return, ready to work.

She didn't want to get married. She didn't want to sort through garbage to find resources. Even more so, she didn't want to capitulate to her father and take the stupid test again. So... what *did* she want to do?

A knock on the bathroom door and her father's voice pushed away her thoughts. "I need to talk to you before I go to work."

She wanted to say plenty to him too, but it wouldn't get them anywhere. She clamped her lips together as if he could see her refusal to speak through the door.

He rapped again. "*Now*, Lexi."

Which was worse? Being stuck in her father's home or being with a stranger the Imperium expected her to wed? "*Fine.*" She spit the word out as if it had been snake venom, then realized how it sounded. She took a cleansing breath. "Give me a second."

She tucked the necklace into her uniform. *Don't pick a fight.*

Be calm and polite.

Her father waited in the kitchen, a half-eaten protein bar in his hand. "I know you're moving out soon, but I don't want you to think you aren't welcome to visit anytime."

Words floated on the tip of her tongue. Words Mom would've been furious to know Lexi even contemplated saying. She sucked her lips into her mouth to keep the words from escaping.

He came around the kitchen island as if he wanted to hug her.

Not going to happen. She backed away.

Red patches blotched his neck, and a low growl emanated from him. "You should know I've been assigned a new wife. Rumi will move in tomorrow."

Rumi? Tomorrow? Lexi couldn't breathe. The room temperature had to have risen. Dizzy, she gripped the counter and forced the bile down. "I gotta go."

She ran to the door, not even pausing when he shouted for her to stop.

Her thoughts roiled. How could he? He could have waited until the mourning period ended to put his request in. The Imperium wouldn't have assigned him to the dorms until then. Heat burned through her stomach.

Lexi ran, bumping off walls and grabbing for handrails to steady herself. Once inside the elevator, she paced in circles, waiting for it to reach its destination. She didn't still until she stood inside the greenhouse on the top floor. Her heart raced as if a madman had chased her.

Time for self-assessment.

Time to woman up.

Life would never return to what it had been.

She allowed the sunlight's warmth and the greenhouse aromas to calm her as they always did. The word *betrayal* bounced around in her head. Mom was gone. Lexi had passed into legal adulthood. Dad no longer owed anything to anyone. He was an adult and could choose to remarry if he wanted. Right?

No. It wasn't right. He needed to mourn Mom for as long as the hole in Lexi's heart took to mend—longer.

A butterfly fluttered past her nose. She loved the insects the Imperium preserved in the greenhouse for pollination. A brief glimpse of nature.

The air hung heavy with moisture from the hydroponics fluids evaporating but unable to escape through the glass ceiling and walls. She pulled it into her lungs, and the weight of it grounded her. If only she could live among the plants.

A young woman came through wearing the green uniform from the Growers' buildings. She couldn't have been much older than seventeen. Her red hair stood out against the green plants, and her speckled cheeks revealed her time working in the sun. She set to work with a testing kit. The girl dipped a tube into the hydroponics and filled it with water, then added drops of fluid from another bottle and shook the mixture. Once it darkened with the movement, she compared the color to a chart.

Sunlight glinted off a silver chain on her neck. When she bent over to toss the contents of the tube into a potted plant, the bobble on the end of the necklace slipped out of her uniform.

Lexi gasped. It was the same locket her mother had given her. Was it possible the girl knew about Y? She looked too innocent to be a rebel.

The girl glanced Lexi's way, then followed Lexi's gaze to the necklace. She shoved the ornament back into her clothing and hustled away.

At first, Lexi stood rooted to the spot, uncertain whether what she'd seen had any meaning. After all, the Imperium made duplicates of everything. Why wouldn't there be multiple copies of the necklace Mom had given her? But if that were the case, why hadn't Lexi seen the same piece of jewelry on lots of other women? Mom insisted it came from the old days, before the war.

She had to find out what it meant before she missed her chance. With quick steps, she hurried down the aisle and spun left and searched for telltale red hair among the few green-uniformed workers. Her heart grew more frantic with each passing second. Where had the girl gone?

The creak of a metal door opening caught her attention, and she saw the back of the girl's head as she left via the maintenance exit. Lexi ran to catch the door before it closed. Relief flooded through her when her fingers blocked it before it could seal. She didn't have security permissions to enter the maintenance areas.

She slipped through and let the door click shut. Light, rapid footsteps sounded in the stairwell, growing fainter. It was twelve flights down. Still sore from the explosion, would she see the girl again if she ran back to the elevators? Probably not. Plus, she didn't have any way to get back into the maintenance area.

Lexi took off down the stairwell. She had to ask about the necklace.

Her lungs begged for oxygen by the time she reached the ground floor and came out of the stairwell door into a hallway. She stopped and held her breath for an agonizing second to listen for footfalls. Silence confirmed she'd lost her.

Gulping air, she searched the area. She had three door options. Two were certain to lead into the interior, but a third, at the far end, most likely led outside. She ran and opened it with caution. The last thing she needed was to end up in a room full of green uniforms while she wore her brown. Nothing like drawing attention to the fact that she was out and about where she didn't belong.

Excitement mixed with trepidation when she encountered the outside world. She'd only been outside one time in her entire life, but the rumors claimed people lived in the Favela. Individuals who didn't fit into the Imperium mold or refused to conform. Poor, hungry, filthy rejections. A teacher once mentioned that many were mentally unstable and unable to live harmoniously in an organized culture. Dangerous.

She stepped through to the outside world. The smell of unwashed bodies and decay seemed out of place with the sunshine now beating on the broken sidewalks. A lump of tattered clothing and blankets rested beside the doorway. When it coughed, Lexi jumped and screeched. The noise caused the bundle to move, and two bloodshot eyes looked out from under the pile, then escaped back underneath the ragged blanket.

Her heart pounded in her throat. What was she doing out here in the street? She didn't belong here. The door clicked shut, and the shock rattled her. That entrance was the only way she knew back inside the Imperium buildings. And she didn't have security access to open it. What an idiot.

Now, she had no other option except to find the redhead. The thought of walking through the Favela on her own made her want to vomit. She clasped the locket hanging from her neck in her sweaty palm. The hair on her nape stood on end. Someone was watching her—she felt it.

The lump of a person remained under the rags. People milled around a burn barrel farther down the sidewalk. Perhaps the redhead had joined that group. Did Lexi dare approach them to ask? Or should she stay by the door and hope someone would come through it soon? What if no one did? A shudder ran through her. She couldn't be locked outside at night. Not with the stories of violence she'd heard about the Favela.

Stop it. You're being stupid. Just go ask them.

Her feet moved of their own volition. It was broad daylight. No one would attack her out in the open.

The closer she came to the people, the stronger the scent grew. Who knew what burned in the barrel, but whatever it was, it stunk. Bad. One of the larger bodies was male, even though stringy, oil-slicked hair hung long down his back. He had to be at least six and a half feet tall, and broad shoulders took up every inch of the green fabric that must have once been a gardener's pristine uniform.

Dirty faces turned toward her, roving over her like spotlights inspecting every inch. No one said anything until she'd entered their small circle. Then a woman with frizzy, knotted hair spoke. "What's a Reclamation doing down here? Don't think you'll find much in the way of resources that we've not already burned."

Their laughter allowed Lexi to relax enough to twitch one side of her mouth upward. "I'm looking for a girl I followed. A redhead. Gardener."

The man in the tattered green outfit frowned. "Why'd you follow her? You don't belong here."

She swallowed the lump rising in her throat. "I wanted to

ask her a question, that's all."

The knotted-hair woman squinted at Lexi. "Must be a pretty important question if you're willing to follow her out here."

Lexi nodded with vigor. "It is. It's about my mom. She died."

The woman's eyes softened. "I'm sorry to hear that." She backhand swatted the giant in tattered green clothing. "Fletcher, go fetch Janie."

Fletcher glared back. "But she's Imperium. We don't know we can trust her." He shook a finger at Lexi's wrist. "She's even wearing a watch. Idiot."

With obvious authority, the woman raised her chin. "Now, Fletcher."

After a brief humph, he spun and stormed away.

Hands on her hips now, the woman rocked back on her heels. "You shouldn't wear a watch here. You know the Imperium tracks your movements, right? The watch tells them where you are." She swept a strand of tangled hair behind an ear. "Let me see that necklace of yours."

A shiver ran through Lexi. She hadn't thought about the watch, though she'd known it had a tracker in it. Stupid move. Even more so, why hadn't she hidden her necklace? If she lost the pendant, she'd never forgive herself. But on the chance the woman wanted to help, Lexi stepped closer to allow her to inspect the locket.

The woman reached out, but when Lexi flinched, she backed off and didn't touch the necklace. "Family heirloom?"

Lexi tucked the locket back into her uniform. "It belonged to my grandmother, then my mom."

Soon Fletcher returned with the redhead in tow. Once they approached the knotted-hair woman, she draped an arm around the girl. "This here's Janie. She works as a gardener for the Imperium but slips out to help in the Favela now and again."

The woman thumped her chest. "I'm Ms. Becky. I sort of manage this area of the Favela." She hooked a thumb toward the big guy. "And of course, you've already met Fletcher, our local grump."

Lexi smiled, then replaced the look with a neutral face in response to the hulking man's scowl.

Ms. Becky's brief smile didn't quite reach her eyes. "And now would you care to introduce yourself?"

Discomfort made her skin itch. How much was too much to share? "I'm Lexi."

Ms. Becky motioned with one hand, beckoning for more. "Lexi…?"

Go big or go home. "Lexi Verity."

Ms. Becky revealed every yellowed tooth she still possessed. "I suspected as much. You must be Tora's daughter. Right? I can see her look on your face. Same nose. Same smile."

A chill ran through Lexi. "You knew my mother?"

Janie stood stoically beside Ms. Becky until now. "But…"

An elbow to the side from Ms. Becky ended the thought before it could even begin. "Yes. We all knew your mama. She'd bring food sometimes to help us out."

Lexi placed her hand on her heart, resting it on the slight bump the pendant created under her uniform. "Janie. Where'd you get your locket? It looks like the one my mom gave me."

Before Janie could get a word out, Ms. Becky jumped in. "Just like yours, Janie inherited an heirloom."

There must be more to the story, but unless Lexi could get Janie away from Ms. Becky, more details wouldn't likely come. Besides, she couldn't blurt out "show me your rebel sign" and expect show-and-tell to begin. She'd need to find another way.

A shrill whistle drew everyone's attention. Janie's eyes went wide, and Ms. Becky nodded. "Sounds like we're getting a visit from the Imperium's Freedom Force. Best they don't find you here."

The surrounding people scattered and disappeared down alleyways. Ms. Becky pointed at Lexi as she spoke to Janie. "You get back inside. Take Lexi with you and make sure she's safe."

"Yes, ma'am." Janie gave a quick nod, then grabbed Lexi's arm, and ran back to the Administration building, dragging Lexi along.

Chapter 9

Nana's pillow lay wedged behind Lexi's back after a night of fitful sleep. Thoughts of the Favela and her lost family members wouldn't let her mind rest.

This was it. Day five. The last official day of mourning for Mom, Nana, and Gramps.

She allowed herself to wallow in self-pity. After pulling the pillow free from her back, she pressed her nose to it and drew in a deep breath. Even with the deepest inhalation, she couldn't capture Nana's scent anymore. They hadn't been gone long enough for her perfume residue to have vanished, but since she'd lain with it all night, her nose had grown accustomed to its odor.

The hole in her chest ached. She wanted to wrap her arms around Gramps or giggle over secrets with Nana. She'd even welcome a scolding from Mom right now.

She huffed out a laugh. If a reprimand was all she needed, she simply had to walk out of the bedroom. Her father would be ready and waiting this morning.

Once she'd returned from the Favela, she'd hidden in her grandparents' bedroom, even after she'd heard her father come in.

He'd knocked on the bedroom door. "Lexi. You in there?"

Her single-word response had been all he'd deserved. "Yeah."

The three words he'd spoken next were enough to keep her locked in the bedroom for the rest of the evening. "Come meet Rumi."

Not. Going. To happen.

Thankfully, he'd given up. Through the thin walls, she'd heard him explain her behavior. "It's been hard for her since she lost her mother and grandparents."

Sure. That was it. Had nothing to do with her father remarrying while he was still in mourning.

Now that dawn had arrived, she contemplated her options. She could hide in this room for the rest of her life, but that was an obvious nonstarter. Food and bodily functions would force an exit, probably before the Imperium had an opportunity to drag her away for being mentally unstable.

She could also escape back to her new apartment. Would Reeves expect the honeymoon to start if she showed up a day early? No sense wasting her last twenty-four hours of freedom.

A growl emanated from her stomach. *Why didn't I eat before I hid last night?* Maybe it would be her lucky day and she could get up and out of the apartment before her father and Rumi rose.

Lexi dressed in the brown uniform and tucked the necklace inside the front. She padded into the kitchen on tiptoes and retrieved a protein bar. The rattle of the wrapper could've woken the dead, even though she ripped it back in slow motion.

She took one giant bite and stuffed the rest into a pocket. With quick steps, she moved to the bathroom to take care of her morning necessities. While she was washing her hands, the crinkle of a wrapper followed footfalls in the kitchen.

Shoot. Not fast enough.

She couldn't let the day start with a fight. She glared at her reflection.

You don't need to argue. You could be nice today.

Good plan. She sucked in a cleansing breath, then exited the bathroom with a grin in place.

A girl no older than Lexi stared at her from the kitchen. Straight ebony hair hung to her tiny waist. If the girl reached five feet in height, Lexi'd eat her socks. She mustn't have been raised in the Administration building, or Lexi would've seen her in school.

Lexi's tongue froze in her mouth as potential conversation starters zoomed through her head.

Slept with my father lately?

No.

Any babies yet?

Nope.

How does it feel to be stuck with a guy twice your age?

Probably inappropriate.

The long-haired waif swallowed down a swig of water. "I'm Rumi, and I assume you're Lexi?"

Captain Obvious, reporting for duty.

Lexi eyed the water glass in Rumi's hand as her own throat went bone dry. "Yeah. Where are you from? I don't recall seeing you in any of my classes."

The girl's eyes lit up as if Lexi said something funny. "Good one. I'm nineteen. Many people think I'm younger. It's because I'm height challenged."

Nineteen? Lexi's eyebrows crinkled as she jammed her hands into her jumpsuit pockets. "Uh-huh."

Rumi moved toward Lexi with arms extended.

Did she think they were going to hug?

Retreating a few steps, Lexi put her hand out as if she were attempting to stop traffic. "That doesn't explain where you're from or why you weren't married off at seventeen."

The glow on Rumi's face vanished as if someone had flipped a switch. "I came from the Orange building. You know, Production?" She held the rest of the protein bar out toward Lexi. "But I scored high enough on the tests to get into Engineering. Two extra years of school. Nice, huh?"

Lexi returned the frown. "I gotta go."

"Oh." Rumi stepped back as if slapped. "What should I tell your dad?"

A laugh barked out of Lexi's mouth before the thought formed in her brain. "Tell him I said goodbye."

She rushed back to the bedroom, threw everything she'd removed into her pack, and fled.

Thoughts of her dad with Rumi brought the food she'd eaten up to burn her throat. She forced herself to swallow it back down. No way was she going to hang out with her father and the new Mrs. Verity. Lexi would happily marry Reeves and take on his name just to rid herself of her father's.

Without thinking about a destination, she escaped to the one place that always centered her. The greenhouse.

The sun beat down on her as warm as her mother's embrace. There were only three people in her life she wanted to hug, though, and she'd never see any of them again.

She wandered the aisles while green-uniformed workers tested water samples, harvested strawberries and spinach leaves, and swept the walkways between the plants. The warm, moist air weighed in her lungs, pulling her back to earth and centering her.

Out of the corner of her eye, she saw a flash of red hair near the exit door. Janie.

Lexi hadn't had time to question the girl after she'd let her back into the Administration building. Now was her chance to find out more about Y. She hurried to catch the door and got her toe in before it closed. Before exiting the greenhouse, she removed her watch and stashed it behind a large plant. *Now try to track me.*

Confident she could move about in secret, she followed the retreating footsteps. Rather than alerting Janie to her presence, she'd see what a rebel got up to during the day. But Janie wasn't headed the same way she'd gone. What was she doing this time?

Down several connecting hallways, Janie led Lexi through the maintenance corridors to an exit door. Lexi kept far enough behind so as not to alert her, yet close enough to catch the door before it closed. Once she'd waited for a beat, she peeked through to see Janie slinking along the outside walkway. She had flipped a hood over her head as she crept toward a camera aimed down one of the air bridges.

Janie slid a can out of her pocket and aimed it at the lens. A purple mist clouded in front of the camera. The screech of an alarm sounded, but instead of fear, the girl's lips twitched upward.

Then Janie dashed onto the air bridge and painted the ornamental Y in the shape of a bird. Wow, the girl was wasting her artistic abilities on tagging buildings. The bird's beauty almost made Lexi wish it could fly off the wall.

A group of Freedom Force soldiers stepped out of a nearby elevator, interrupting her distracted thought. They raised their weapons as they hollered. "Citizen, stop!"

Janie tore off down the hallway, away from the gun-wielding

police, and toward Lexi's hiding spot.

The girl ran at the speed of the young and nimble, but the Freedom Force guards, even weighed down with their weapons and bulletproof shielding, were gaining on her.

An officer near the front of the group got close enough to shoot a Taser, but only one prong connected. Instead of receiving the jolt of electricity two connections would provide, Janie broke free while the prong, minus the wire, remained in her shoulder.

Too close. They'd have her soon.

Janie neared the door. Lexi couldn't sit idle and let the soldiers catch the girl. Instead, the moment Janie reached the door, Lexi swung it open to allow Janie free access. She whispered "I'll hold them off" as the girl passed her. While Janie sped past, Lexi feigned confusion and twirled into the hallway, arms wide, blocking the pursuers. "What? What happened?"

The first pursuer tripped over her, flipping onto his back, his weapon flying free. Curses spewed from the soldiers. "Get out of the way."

While she tried to make it look like she was getting up, she did her best to block as many as she could from following Janie. At last, one man yanked her out of the way, jarring her shoulder. "Ouch."

The soldier glared at her. "What are you up to? I should charge you with obstruction of justice."

No way would she tick off the Freedom Force. Anyone who did suffered the consequences. She cast her gaze toward the floor and slumped her shoulders. "Sorry. You caught me off guard. I didn't realize you were chasing someone. I can describe what she looked like."

The officer's eyes went wide. "It was a girl? You saw her

without the mask?"

Shoot. Said too much. She raised her eyebrows as if shocked by the question. "No. But the person seemed not much taller than I am or maybe a little shorter. Wouldn't that make her a girl? And she wore a green uniform and a black mask."

He shoved her away. "We saw that much. What good are you? Get back to your building before I make good on that obstruction charge."

She shrank back, her gaze on the floor. "Yes… yes, sir."

Grateful for the chance to flee, she trotted off toward the elevator. It wouldn't be safe to hang around the Administrative building any longer today. Not that it mattered. She had no interest in going back to her father's apartment and making nice with Rumi. That left her with one remaining option—her new apartment in Reclamation. *Time to face my future.*

What were the chances Reeves would be out tonight? Perhaps one last night with his parents before the big day tomorrow? It could happen.

After she'd retrieved her watch from the rooftop greenhouse, the ride to the Reclamation building ended before she could collect her thoughts. Images of the rebel symbol competed for dominance against thoughts of what marriage would be like. If her mother had been a rebel, why hadn't she known about the bomb? What would Reeves think if he found out about Lexi's mom? Should she join the rebels and follow in her mother's footsteps? Mom believed in the cause enough to risk her life. People should have the freedom to choose.

She found herself in front of her new home. Her forced future.

It had been inevitable. The Imperium expected everyone to conform. *Unity above all else.* She was legally an adult now, her job in Reclamation only part of the picture. They expected her to marry and produce children. Repopulate. *A young Imperium is a thriving Imperium.*

She placed her palm on the security screen, and the door clicked open. "Reeves? You home?"

Silence. The place was hers, for now. Her shoulders relaxed.

In the bedroom, she slid open the top dresser drawer, pulled her clothes out of the backpack, and stuffed them into their new home. Looking around the spartan room, she wandered to the bed and sat down with the cookbook in her lap. After she scooted to rest her back against the headboard, she dropped the diary out of its hiding place and opened it to where she'd left off.

She could almost read between the lines. Mom wrote sporadically for a few weeks. One sentence here and there was about how Lexi grew, slept, and even what she ate. It appeared as though Lexi had consumed her mother's entire world for those months.

The Imperium valued children and granted women six months of maternity leave to care for their newborns and recuperate from the childbirth process. At the one-year mark, they gave both parents a month off with free day care as a birthday present. Everyone knew the expectation for baby number two to be conceived on or soon after that anniversary vacation.

She'd sketched a birthday cake in the corner of one page, next to the words *Happy Birthday, Baby Lexi.* Mom wrote Lexi's weight, height, and favorite food—green beans.

There were notes about evenings when Lexi stayed in the day care unit so her parents could attend official Administration gatherings. These entries intermingled with comments about

Lexi's first steps, then her first word—*mama*.

Every month there were doctor visits, each with a frown face drawn beside it. After six of the sad-face entries, Lexi found a detailed account.

> *Had my six-month follow-up with the doctor today. They'd done more in-depth testing since Gunner insisted on a second opinion. Still no good news. I'm tired of never being enough for my husband, and I'm sick to death of him ignoring the daughter we have.*

The next entry made Lexi's blood boil.

> *Gunner has turned cold toward both Lexi and me. He blames me for my sterility and her for causing it. As if either of us controlled the situation. I'm grateful to have our sweet child, but all he cares about is that she's the only one. Why can't he appreciate what we've got, instead of being angry over what will never be?*

How dare he treat Mom that way? Lexi wouldn't be shocked if she found out her father was relieved Mom had died. Now he could marry again and have all those babies he'd wanted the first time around. Bonus—Nana and Gramps were with Mom, so her father wouldn't have to kick anyone out to have the apartment alone with his new woman.

Lexi itched to go back home to tell him what she thought of him. She set the diary aside. Mom's anguished thoughts made Lexi antsy, and she paced around the bedroom, uncertain what to do with the frustration buildup.

She would never cave to what the Imperium wanted. If the

rebels behind Y were going to fight the status quo, then she was on board.

One problem—today was her last day of mourning. Tomorrow, she'd be the new bride. Expected to enjoy her honeymoon and start making babies with Reeves. Her hands fisted with a desire to punch someone or something. This was beyond unfair. It was wrong. How was she going to get through the wedding without landing herself in prison?

Chapter 10

The buzz of Lexi's watch jerked her out of the nightmare. Her sodden shirt stuck to her as she swatted the alarm into silence. Images from the dream lingered. Mom, Nana, and Gramps smiling as the world burned down around them. *No. They aren't suffering anymore. They're good.*

She disentangled her limbs from the twisted blanket and sheets. Thoughts of cold water beckoned her out of bed. Paste stuck her swollen tongue against the roof of her mouth. The hum of the neighbors' discussion floated through the thin walls of her otherwise silent apartment.

Padding out to the kitchen, she let out a squeak at the sight of a man on the pullout bed. Reeves. How'd he get in without her hearing him? His sleep-disheveled hair pointed in all directions at once while drool clung to the corner of his mouth. With his eyes closed in slumber, he looked much younger than his seventeen years.

But he hadn't assumed any marital rights and joined her in bed. He hadn't even awoken her. If the Imperium doomed her to be stuck with a guy of their choosing, she could have done much worse.

A message alert flashed on her watch. She scrolled to read it on the one-inch screen and rolled her eyes at the words.

The Imperium wishes you a pleasant wedding day. Please report promptly for your marriage health assessment at 0900 in Reproductive Health. Your attendance is mandatory. May your union be productive. One marriage—many children.

Of all the slogans the Imperium shoved down her throat, she hated that one the most today. Reeves's watch alert was on as well. Should she wake him and point it out?

Nope. The Imperium made sure their messages didn't go unread for long, and they didn't require any help from her.

A box of protein bars waited on the counter. Reeves must have picked some up, and for that, she was grateful. It seemed odd to help herself to food she hadn't purchased, in a home that didn't feel like her own. But the next week would be full of firsts.

Her heart twisted. If only Mom could be here.

The crinkle of the wrapper sounded loud. She took a bite and stared at Reeves, expecting him to wake.

His watch flashed red, the telltale sign of an unread message warning. A buzz emanated from the device. How could he sleep so sound that he didn't realize he'd gotten an alert? She'd never forget the first time she'd gotten a shock from her watch after ignoring the warnings for too long. Ever since, she'd caught herself checking for messages when she'd even imagined a vibration. This should be fun. She counted down.

Three... two... one...

Reeves sprang up, shaking his wrist while she smirked. No one ignored an official Imperium message for long.

He pulled up the memo, read it, then looked around, his eyes blurry.

At least she wasn't the only person feeling out of place.

"Morning."

His sleep-filled eyes blinked at her, trying to focus. Then he flopped back down. "Morning." The word came out thick, his mouth probably as pasty as hers had been.

Seeing him in such a natural state made her heart lurch. He wasn't the enemy. They were both cogs in the Imperium's baby-making machine. She picked up a protein bar and tossed it to him. "I'm heading out for my exam. You might want to get moving."

He slammed a pillow over his eyes, then raised one hand, and waved at her. A silent farewell. A bitter taste filled her mouth. How she hated that she was starting to like this guy.

When she arrived at Reproductive Health, Aponi in the waiting room surprised her. Aponi's nuptials were over, so she had to be past this part of the Imperium's tests.

Lexi placed her palm on the attendant screen to inform the office she'd arrived, then took a seat next to her friend. "What are you doing here?"

Aponi slumped back, her face pale and her eyebrows knitted together. "Not sure yet. I got a call to come back in." She huffed out a laugh, but her gaze clung to Lexi's. "We're not even past the honeymoon. It's way too early to test."

The pregnancy evaluations would start early and happen often for a newlywed wife. Everyone knew the pressure to conceive the first baby would grow exponentially with each passing month. If too many months went by without success, the husband would get hauled into the testing cycle as well.

Lexi had never heard of anyone having an exam during their honeymoon, though. It had to be something else. Her best friend couldn't be having issues. Lexi's throat went dry. She squeezed her friend's shoulder. "I'm sure it's just some sort of technicality. You probably forgot to sign something in triplicate."

Aponi glanced at the door to the evaluation rooms. "Yeah, it's gotta be something stupid like that."

Wanting to assure her friend everything would be okay in the end, Lexi twisted sideways in her chair. Perhaps a change of subject could give Aponi a chance to ooze happiness over her new mate. "So how's it going? You enjoying married life?" Lexi rolled her eyes. "Is he still your dreamboat?"

Aponi rewarded her with a smile. "He's a great guy. If you gave him half a chance, you'd like him." She tilted her head to the side and smirked. "You know, you don't need to be so independent all the time. You might find out someone special can fill in your holes. Make you more solid than you can be on your own."

As if I need someone else to make me whole. Aponi had gone all in with the Imperium's propaganda.

Both jumped when a nurse bellowed. "Lexi Verity?"

Lexi gave Aponi's hand a quick squeeze. "I hope it's nothing. Wish me luck." Then she followed the nurse, her nerves buzzing with the desire to flee.

After the health aid recorded her weight, measurements, and vitals, she handed Lexi a hospital gown and told her to get undressed and wait in the exam chair. This part always caused Lexi's heart to beat out of control. She wished she could crawl under the chair instead.

Gynecological exams occurred every year since the day she turned twelve, as if the Imperium needed to ensure their incubators were growing properly. She never got used to the invasion and hated being a woman more than anything, if only because they forced the inspection on her.

Like a whipped dog, she followed orders, shed her clothing, and donned the gown. Being nude in the cold, sterile environment left her more exposed than if she stood naked in front of a firing squad. Her heart hammered as she climbed on the frigid table and placed her feet into the steel stirrups. She wanted to scream at the indignity.

A doctor stepped into the room, focused on his tablet. He set the device on a table, sat on a short, rolling stool, then sidled in between Lexi's knees to inspect her. Without a word, he pushed and pressed her inside and out with painful force. She might as well have been a specimen in a lab under his rough treatment.

He pulled away, ending the assault, then smacked her hip with his palm. "You've got good hips. Shouldn't have any trouble with childbirth. Wish I could say that about more of our women. Too many have narrow hips these days. Hard for the babies to pass through." Then he walked out of the room, mumbling to himself.

His callous words escalated the sense of violation. Her cheeks burned as she rushed to get back into her clothes. She threw the absurd gown across the room. It hit the wall and slid down into the corner. Let them yell at her if they didn't want her dressed. She'd had enough.

A phlebotomist came into the room next with a tray of empty tubes and a scowl marring what would have been a pretty face. "What'd you dress for? We're not done."

Lexi rolled her sleeve up above her elbow, then thrust her arm out. "My arm is naked enough."

With a growl, the woman set the tray on the bed and wrapped a rubber tube around Lexi's left biceps.

It was the tightest Lexi had ever experienced. That was

a mistake. She shouldn't have shown attitude to the person about to jab her with needles.

By the time the phlebotomist finished, eight blood-filled tubes lined the box. The woman grumbled while Lexi yanked her sleeve back down. "You can go now. We'll send a message if we need more."

More? If they took much more, she'd need a transfusion. Not wanting to stay in the room a moment longer, she fled out the door and down the hallway.

Once she'd gotten far enough from the health unit, her heart calmed back to a normal rhythm. A glimpse of her watch informed her she had some time to kill before the wedding. If any of her family, besides her father, were still alive, she'd have spent the time with them.

If Mom and Nana were still alive, they'd share stories of their wedding days. They'd all wait together for the event—not that there was much to an Imperium ceremony. Her father probably knew about the nuptials, even though Lexi hadn't felt the need to tell him. If it meant that much to him, he'd use his security clearance to get the information and show up. Not that it mattered. This wasn't a day for celebration. Not for her.

What about Reeves and his family? What would her in-laws be like? Dad's parents retired to Solitude when his mom got too sick to work, so Lexi never met them. As was typical with the challenges related to childbearing since the war, both Mom and Dad had been only children, so there were no aunts or uncles. Hers would be a quiet service.

She twisted her hands into fists. With her remaining hours, she wanted to find Janie and ask her questions. There were so many questions. Why hadn't she thought of it sooner?

It couldn't have been more obvious where she needed to head. The greenhouse. Janie still worked there, if the Imperium hadn't tracked her down yet.

Within a half hour of leaving her tormentors behind, all the stress had leached from Lexi's body. Once more, the sun shone through the glass ceiling and warmed her skin. Scents of earth, water, and strawberries tantalized her nose. The distraction threatened to derail her plan to find Janie. *Focus. You don't have time to dawdle.*

Methodically, she walked aisle by aisle, looking for telltale red hair. Would she find the girl before her time ran out?

Aha, there. Janie squatted on a wheeled stool, picking strawberries.

Lexi rushed over and tapped Janie's shoulder. "Hey. Can we talk?"

Janie's eyes widened as she turned. Once she recognized Lexi, she twitched her head toward the maintenance exit. When they reached the door, Janie pointed at Lexi's watch.

Right. After stashing the device behind the potted plant, Lexi tailed Janie into the quiet hallway. Then, eager to get her questions answered, Lexi started to rapid fire them the moment the door closed. "Can you connect me with Y? Is Ms. Becky the leader? I need to know if my mom was a member."

With a glare, Janie hissed, "Shh." She pointed at her ear, then her eye, then down the hallway.

She must think I'm an idiot. Who knew what cameras were in the area and what the Imperium could hear?

Lexi followed Janie down the path they'd taken to exit the Administration building and join the homeless people in the Favela.

Outside, Janie gripped Lexi's arm. "Look. I appreciate how

you saved my butt. I owe you. Big time."

Lexi opened her mouth to request some quid pro quo, but Janie put a hand up to silence her.

With a headshake, Janie lowered the hand. "I don't have any answers for you, but I know who does. If you give me some time, I can arrange a meeting. But you need to understand, it's dangerous. Anyone found collaborating with Y is in as much danger as a member."

Nana had told Lexi stories of bobblehead dolls from before the war, and Lexi had to look like one now. She couldn't agree to the terms fast and fervently enough. "I get it. I'm not afraid. Just get me that meeting."

Janie's eyebrows furrowed. "You're a fool if you're *not* terrified. I am. But that won't stop us. We won't quit until we break the Imperium and its corrupt control over the people."

Lexi's heart rate ticked upward. She'd never done anything this crazy before, but if it brought her any closer to understanding her mother, it would be worth it. She had to know. "I'm in. Just tell me what to do, and I'll do it."

"Give me until tomorrow. Meet me at the strawberry patch again first thing in the morning. Don't be late. I've got assignments I can't leave undone, and I'm not waiting."

Tomorrow would be her first official day of married life. They didn't have to go to work as they'd be on their honeymoon. But would she be able to ditch Reeves that soon? Didn't matter. No way would she miss this chance. Even if she had to get up at two in the morning to get away from him, she'd make it work. She had to know. "I'll be there."

A round of gunfire went off south of their location. A group of Favela homeless were running. An enormous man led them. Fletcher. More gunshots rang out, closer this time.

Wide-eyed, Janie grabbed Lexi's sleeve. "Come on. You need to get out of here."

The lump in Lexi's throat threatened to choke off her airway as they spun to the door. What were the chances she'd end up in prison before she even had time to find the rebels? Janie's palm slapped the security pad, and the door clicked, freeing the lock.

Lexi shuddered as Janie pushed her through the doorway. "They'll know you were out here." Lexi stopped in the stairwell. "Your palm access—it'll give you away."

Janie jabbed Lexi in the back, prodding her to keep moving. "It's rigged to push back the palm of a dead Y member if the Freedom Force ever looks it up. They just don't know he's dead yet."

They slipped into the humid, sunlit greenhouse. *"You* get out of here. *I'm* going back to work. Don't forget. Tomorrow. Strawberry patch. 0800."

Janie stepped through the door with a glance backward before shutting it.

"I'll be there." Lexi retrieved her watch. *Shoot.* She'd wasted more time than she'd planned.

She sped toward the Administration's marriage registration office. The last thing she needed was for a Freedom Force alert to go out to find her because she didn't show up for the wedding. People who didn't cooperate with the process ended up homeless in the Favela—or worse.

She was out of breath by the time she gripped the doorknob that would lead her past the point of no return. Reeves would be inside—waiting. She checked her watch. Ten minutes late. Not a great start to their relationship.

When she stepped into the office, he jumped from the

waiting room chair. His dirty-blond hair, still wet from a shower, had been slicked back. His lips stretched upward. "Had me worried there."

She worked to slow her breathing. "Sorry. Lost track of time."

A middle-aged woman with thick glasses and even thicker eyebrows stood behind a counter. A glass partition with a slot at the bottom and a speaker box in the middle separated her office from the waiting room. She spoke in a no-nonsense tone. "Ms. Verity, I presume?"

Her cheeks burned under the woman's glare. "Yes, ma'am."

The woman pointed toward a palm reader alongside the partition. "Scan in."

With a deep breath, Lexi moved to the scanner and pressed her palm to the double-wide panel. Reeves placed his hand beside hers, which activated the scan.

As if she'd said the words a million times already today, the woman droned out her speech. "Do you both swear to be faithful to the Imperium and your relationship? Do you swear to strive for as many children as possible to strengthen the population of the Imperium? And do you understand that any unfaithful acts against your spouse or toward the Imperium may result in disciplinary action, up to and including imprisonment, expulsion, or corporal punishment?"

A lump filled Lexi's throat. Reeves had grown pale. Their response came out in unison. "I do."

Chapter 11

The walk back to the transport area might as well have been a march to Lexi's death. The words from the ceremony, if you could call it that, sank into her consciousness like a millstone. Neither of them spoke as they walked side-by-side as if the Imperium watched them and gauged their willingness to copulate.

Was every eye focusing on them? Tingles crawled along her skin. The whole world knew their new status and must wonder if they'd start making babies on the tram ride back to their apartment. Her hands had gone cold and clammy. This entire situation was so wrong.

The Imperium shouldn't have forced her to marry at seventeen, much less assigned her mate. They called their enforcers the Freedom Force, but she wasn't free. Neither was Reeves. He shouldn't be the target of her frustration, but that didn't keep her from wanting to run from him.

As the tram neared the Brown building, she stole a sideways glance at her new husband, sitting next to her on the bench, his eyes wide and glassy, as if in a trance. Before the ceremony, he'd been almost flippant. Now his face had gone pale, and sweat trickled down his cheek from the flock of beads crowning his forehead. He wasn't much different from her.

Somehow, the obvious shock in his eyes made her own all that more bearable. She wasn't in this by herself—not completely.

They exited the tram and trudged to the elevators, then off at their floor. The walk down the hallway to their front door felt as if they were on parade. Were people watching them from their hallway monitors? She scowled at the corridor full of door cams. None moved, but all had green lights glowing. No one was ever truly alone.

She wanted this day to be over. To be past their first night together. She wanted to search for answers about Y. To follow Janie and talk to Ms. Becky. Instead, they reached their apartment door and scanned the lock open.

There might as well have been a firing squad waiting for them in the kitchen for as much as she wanted to go inside. Reeves opened the door and went in, his steps robotic. His voice came out not much louder than a whisper. "We're home."

Like it or not, he spoke the truth. This place, until they produced their first child, was home. She followed him into the kitchen, closing the door behind her.

Reeves's was perspiring—a lot. Now that she paid more attention, she noted his breaths were rapid and shallow. "Are you okay?"

He remained silent, his expression vacant.

She touched his arm. His face was white as the Administration building walls. Her heart sped up. "Reeves? I need you to speak to me. Say *something*."

With a nod, he twisted his lips up into a weak smile. "I'm good. It's all good." Then he wobbled.

That did it.

She grabbed his arm and dragged him toward the couch,

then gave him enough of a shove to get him seated. "Wait here."

Back in the kitchen, she selected a glass from the cabinet, filled it, and took it over to him. "Drink."

At first, he sipped at the water, but then guzzled the entire glass as if someone had flipped a switch inside him. Color speckled on his neck, then moved up into his face. The blush looked much better than the pale shock. "Thanks. I feel better. Um, sorry about that."

She flopped beside him, whooshing out her relief. "No problem. I can't say I feel much better."

His eyes squinted, and his brow furrowed. "You're beautiful—you know that?"

Heat burned her cheeks. "Thanks. You're not so hard on the eyes yourself."

He barked out a laugh. "Aren't we a sad excuse for a newlywed couple? I didn't know what to expect, but it wasn't this."

Lexi couldn't keep from smiling. His laugh was infectious. But she needed to be honest. He deserved the truth. "I hate to break it to you, but I'm a rebel at heart. The Imperium shouldn't have the right to force me into a marriage, much less into having a baby."

His eyebrows jerked upward. "We don't get a choice, do we? It's been this way since our great-grandparents fought the final war. You know the history. They didn't have any option but to change the way the world worked. There were too many people living way too long and not enough young people to support them."

She glared at him and folded her arms across her chest. "I took history classes, the same as you. But they've taken it to an extreme. It doesn't have to be this way."

He rolled his eyes. "Come on. You know about the crisis—population, divorce, family. For crying out loud, how else could they fix it, except to mandate forever marriages? At least they figured out how to match people up so we're a good fit."

Heat roiled in her stomach. Reeves had bought into the system. "Can't you see we're missing a key ingredient here?"

With a shrug, he lifted both hands. "What?"

"Love."

He snorted. "Chemical reactions in the brain. You know… you can get a pill for that. The Imperium provides enhancement medications for those who struggle to settle in. You could talk to the doctor at your next appointment. We can wait until then, if it'll make it easier for you."

"What is up with you? Before the ceremony, you acted casual, as if it was no big deal. Then on the way home, you looked like you might pass out from the shock. Now you're back to supporting this ridiculous farce?" Acidic bile churned into her throat, and her knuckles whitened as she balled her hands into fists. "I'm not interested in taking a pill to make me feel the way the Imperium wants me to… something that *should* be natural."

He sighed as if speaking to a petulant child. "It was just a suggestion. You don't have to go all ballistic on me."

Ballistic? The guy didn't have a clue.

She sprang to her feet. "I get it. We're stuck. But I don't have to be happy about it."

"No?" His frustrated tones rose. "By all means, let's be *miserable*."

The temptation to run overwhelmed her. If only she could take off, flee to the greenhouse, find Janie, and hide in the

Favela. How much worse could homelessness be than a forced marriage and a life she didn't want?

Then the unthinkable happened. Her body betrayed her. The anger had built up to where she couldn't hold it back anymore, and it escaped as a tear. *Ugh. Why do I have to cry like a baby?*

She grabbed her backpack and stalked toward the bedroom, searching for a private spot. When she opened the door and saw the enormous bed, she realized her mistake and slammed it shut again.

Reeves got off the couch and joined her. His eyes softened, and he reached out to touch her. "Hey. I'm sorry. It's going to be okay."

His eyes drew her in. It would be so easy to fall into an embrace and accept the only comfort available to her. But if she did that—if she accepted his touch—then the system won. *Not. Going. To happen. Ever.*

She dashed into the only other room she could barricade herself in—the bathroom—and slammed the door. Even if she had to sleep in the tub, she wouldn't leave this room until he was gone.

He stood on the other side of the door. "Lexi, come on. Don't be that way."

It seemed like forever before he gave up and left her hidden away in the tiny room. Sure, her actions were childish, but that didn't propel her out of her quiet spot. She showered. Brushed her teeth. Combed out her wet hair. Pondered her mother's potential involvement with Y. Pulled her tablet out of her backpack and scrolled through screens without taking in their content. Anything to avoid thinking about her husband.

She shivered.

My husband.

The apartment had been quiet for a while when she ventured a peek through the cracked-open door. Lights were out in the living space. Maybe he'd left. She wandered out to the couch, so much like her old bed that she could have been back at home with her parents and grandparents asleep in their rooms.

She spun to the wall where her grandparents' bedroom door would have been. Not there. Just like them.

Overwhelmed by loneliness, she collapsed on top of the cushions and let the tears flow. How was she ever going to get out of this? She wished she'd been with her family when the bomb had disintegrated them. To feel nothing must be better than the ache that had settled into her gut.

Then she thought of Nana. If she were here, she'd give Lexi a lecture on inner strength. She'd never been one to let herself or Lexi wallow in self-pity. Nana would tell her to get busy and *do* something. But what?

Lexi stared at the kitchen appliances. Hers. She doubted whoever cleaned the apartment before they'd assigned it spent much time focused on the appliances. Since people rarely cooked fresh food, they often gave the oven, microwave, and refrigerator only a cursory wipe. That wouldn't cut it for Nana or Mom.

She knew what her mission was. Clean this apartment until they could eat off the floor if they wanted to. After all, this was *her* home, and she needed something to focus on.

Her watch read ten o'clock by the time she'd gathered the supplies and scoured every surface. The aching back she'd earned with the hard work was like a badge of honor, if only she had someone to share the accomplishment with. The realization that she didn't have anyone brought an ache to her chest. Then exhaustion hit her like she'd been run over by a maintenance cart.

Lexi looked at the bedroom door. Nope. Reeves hadn't returned during her marathon cleaning session, but he could be home at any moment. No way would he find her in their marital bed when he did. She'd slept on the pullout for as long as she could remember. No need to change at this point.

Before she allowed herself to drift off to sleep, she set the alarm on her watch. Assuming her husband would come home during the night, she needed to be out of here before Reeves woke and demanded her time and attention. He was a problem for another day.

The alarm's buzz broke into a dream she didn't want to leave. Mom had been there. Nana and Gramps as well. They'd been trying to tell Lexi something, but it had been a secret. Every time they opened their mouths, someone would interrupt them. Then they'd move to find a new spot. Then the cycle would repeat. It hadn't mattered, though. They'd all been with her again. She'd do anything to stay in the dream forever.

With a sigh, she got up. Then she padded to the bathroom, brushed her teeth, and headed back to the kitchen to grab a protein bar. A mumbled voice came from the bedroom. Was Reeves awake this early? She tiptoed over to the door and listened.

More sounds came from the room, all unintelligible. Talking in his sleep. She'd have to get used to that.

She needed to get out of the apartment now before he woke, so she headed for the door. Once she made it to the transportation hub, she took the next tram to the Administration building.

In record time, she stood by the strawberry bed. Her watch told her she was early. Stupid early. She was about to wander away when a tap on her shoulder made her jump, and she let out a squeak.

Janie stood behind her, a finger to her lips to silence Lexi, before she whispered, "It's me."

Lexi whooshed out her breath and lowered her voice. "You scared me to death."

With a roll of her eyes, Janie jutted her chin toward the exit. "Let's go."

Before she knew it, Lexi had ditched her watch, and they'd exited the Administration building. The trash-covered streets were vacant. Not even the homeless lump beside the exit door remained. They stuck to the edges of buildings as if they could climb up the walls at the first sign of trouble.

A tingle ran up Lexi's spine. "Where did everyone go?"

Though there didn't appear to be anyone in the vicinity, Janie still whispered. "It's not safe. The Freedom Force patrols are arresting anyone they catch out on the streets. Rumor is they're executing prisoners."

The lump returned to Lexi's throat, and she swallowed hard against it. "They can't do that without a trial. The news would get out."

Janie paused at the corner, peeked around the edge, then glared at Lexi. "You think the news tells us anything about what actually happens in the Imperium? You're dumber than you look."

Heat rushed to Lexi's cheeks. Until last week, she'd not thought much about Y's mission or the reason for its existence. She had bigger problems than some strange protest group. That was what she thought... until she realized Mom had connections to Y.

She clamped her mouth shut and followed Janie.

They rounded a corner, then ran across an open expanse of a roadway into the shadow of another building.

Someone bellowed. "Stop. Freedom Force."

Then gunfire popped.

Janie grabbed Lexi's arm, yanked her into a doorway, and jiggled the knob—locked. They stood, frozen in the shadows, waiting for whatever came next. But first, Lexi's heart might jump out of her chest. Her breaths came in fast, shallow gasps.

Nearby, the trample of feet hitting pavement and kicking through trash echoed. The footfalls drew closer, and the grunts of runners grew louder. They pressed their backs against the door, and Lexi closed her eyes in the game she'd played as a child. If she couldn't see whatever scared her, then the scary thing couldn't see her. Foolish. Childish.

She reopened them as a man raced into view. The homeless man now wore the filthy blanket she'd seen that first day like a cape, a hole cut into the center for his head to poke free. His eyes were frantic as he made the mistake of turning to look at his pursuers. In that distracted moment, he stepped into a pothole and collapsed to the crumbling asphalt.

Before he could scramble to his feet, two Freedom Force soldiers drew up to his prone body, pulled out Tasers, and shot him. His body convulsed with the electricity's pulse. One soldier spoke into a radio. "We've got one down on Main and Tenth. Send a truck."

After the man's body stopped shaking, his eyes focused on Janie and Lexi. If he alerted his captors of their presence, they had nowhere to run to. Icy cold sluiced through her body. Not even her father's connections could rescue her if they convicted her as a member of Y. She put a hand over her mouth to silence her heavy breaths.

When the man averted his gaze, one officer kicked him. "Don't move, or the next shot will be a bullet to the head."

After an eternity of them hiding in the shadows, the truck arrived. It had probably been only minutes. Two more guards got out, then manhandled their captive into the back.

So, this was what life on the run as a member of Y would be like. Did she still want to know the extent of her mom's involvement?

This was the only path to follow to see if it led to the truth.

No, she didn't want to know—she *had* to know.

Chapter 12

Once the Freedom Force drew away, Lexi scuttled behind Janie, out of their hiding place, and down the trash-littered street. They zigzagged along narrow alleys while listening for soldiers and watching for drones.

Maybe she should've been relieved when Janie pointed to a rusted and bent fire escape stairway that crawled up the side of a building. Instead, her heartbeat quickened even more. "Up there."

The stairs creaked and groaned under their weight. The ancient building would probably crumble into a heap at any moment. Why would Y have chosen this haggard structure when so many others looked much more stable? Ahead of Lexi, Janie stepped through an open window.

Lexi tried to follow when an enormous paw of a hand reached out from the opening and grabbed hold of her wrist. It took every ounce of her courage not to scream when the hand tugged her into the room.

Once her eyes acclimated to the dark interior, she recognized Ms. Becky, her frizzy hair stuffed under a ragged beanie and her smile stretching her thin lips. Janie flanked her. But who had hauled her inside? Ah, Fletcher, with his scowl, towered behind her.

Ms. Becky spoke first, a beatific glow to her features. "Welcome, Lexi. Janie tells me you have… questions."

Lexi wanted to know so much. Everything. But where to start? She shuffled deeper into the dark room with its spatter of broken furniture. "Is this your headquarters?"

A growl from behind told her she'd asked the wrong question. Fletcher snatched at her wrist again, squeezing it like a vise. "I told you. She's up to no good. We need to get rid of her. Now."

Lexi's heart leaped into her throat. Fletcher meant business. She needed to get to her point—fast. "No. Sorry. You don't have to answer that. What I want to know—*need* to know—is how you knew my mom."

Ms. Becky's eyes creased in the corners, and her lips flattened out. "Your mother was a wonderful, caring human being. You must miss her terribly."

The words struck her like an arrow to the heart. Was Ms. Becky being evasive or showing she cared? Lexi jiggled her necklace out from under her uniform, opened the locket, and twisted off the picture. She pointed at the symbol. "Why did she have this? Was she a member of Y? Does Janie's necklace have the same symbol? Was my nana a member?"

Ms. Becky put a hand up to stop the rapid-fire questions, then shook her head at Fletcher, who released the death grip on Lexi's wrist. She waved Lexi over to a threadbare couch where a red brick substituted for one missing leg. "Sit. Let's chat like old friends."

Pinpricks tingled in her fingers as blood flowed through them once again. She glared at Fletcher, then took her seat. Ms. Becky didn't smell like she was homeless. Though her worn clothes had moth holes, the faint scent of soap betrayed recent washing, and the woman's hair wasn't greasy either.

Lexi hated that her next words came out in a pleading tone. "Can you tell me the *truth* about my mom?"

Fletcher growled again and crossed his arms over his chest. His opinion on the subject obvious.

Ms. Becky patted Lexi's knee. A black spot of decay nestled between her two front teeth. No dentists in the poverty-stricken Favela. "I'll tell you what I can. But you need to understand. Every tidbit I share with you about our little rebellion and your mother's involvement puts you in more danger."

Lexi chewed on her lower lip. "I understand, but I *need* to know."

Ms. Becky settled back into the rickety couch. "Don't you find it ironic that the Imperium's guards are called the Freedom Force? Especially since their enforcement is the opposite of freedom?"

Unwilling to stop the flow of information, Lexi nodded but remained silent.

With a glance toward Fletcher, Ms. Becky continued. "After the war and the population collapse, the smartest people still alive realized something had to change. Our country had grown old with too few young adults to support the elderly. Medicine had advanced to where we kept our elders alive until well past the point where they were productive—or even happy."

The history leading up to the war wasn't new to Lexi, though it seemed more real coming from Ms. Becky's point of view.

Ms. Becky patted the other seat beside her, and Janie joined them on the couch. "Not only were fewer people having babies but they also couldn't stop arguing. Fights became our national language. Angry words turned into arguments, then came gunfights. Eventually, civil war broke out. A conflict our country thought would never come again. But it did."

Fletcher moved back to the window ledge and sat. His heavy boots scuffed the floorboards—back and forth, back and forth—while Ms. Becky continued.

"Once our internal squabbles morphed to all-out civil war, we were ripe for the picking by other countries... and pick they did. By the time it was over, the wars had decimated our population again. Most of the casualties were our young people. A generation—gone."

Lexi swallowed hard. "That's why the Imperium forces us to have children. To repopulate. But why impose their selection on us, instead of allowing us to choose our spouses?"

Ms. Becky smoothed out her ragged pant leg. "Before the war, divorce was an immense problem. People knew they could walk away, and they often did. Plus, when people are fighting, they aren't making babies. The Imperium thought their algorithms could match people up better than our hearts could. The only way to force the issue was to mandate it. So, they stole our freedom for the greater good."

Though the history classes hadn't explained things quite so succinctly, none of this was earthshaking news. "What does all of this have to do with Y? What does Y even stand for? How was Mom involved? What about—"

Ms. Becky's hand went into the stop-signal position again. "Not every story is mine to tell. No matter how much I loved your mother, how much I *miss* her, she chose not to share her involvement with you for a reason. I will honor her decision."

Lexi let out a growl as if a feral dog hid within her. "Why did Janie even bring me here if you weren't going to tell me about my mom?"

Fletcher grumbled out a harrumph. He didn't say as much, but his action seemed to voice agreement.

When Ms. Becky eyed him, he broke contact first, making it obvious who was in charge. She let out a breath and crossed her arms over her chest. "That's an excellent question. One we don't all agree on. In my opinion, you've staged a mini rebellion against the Imperium by throwing your test and getting moved to Reclamation."

Lexi's mouth fell open. How could anyone have known about the test? "But I... how? I didn't."

Janie's eyebrows shot up, and her mouth formed an *O*.

With a tilt of her head, Ms. Becky looked at Lexi the way Mom used to when she caught her in a fib. "Your father knows. So does the Imperium. They're turning a blind eye to it, for now. Your father has enough political clout to save you from instant banishment to the Favela for crimes against the Imperium. Who knows how long that grace period will hold out for you? And for him."

A shiver ran through Lexi. She hadn't thought of the consequences to her father if the Imperium realized what she'd done. "What can I do?"

Ms. Becky stood. "The way I see it, you have two choices. You could join Y. We'll protect you as best we can. However, you need to know we risk our lives every day to combat the Imperium's plans. Like Janie, here, who almost got herself caught because she pulled one of her artistic stunts."

Janie lifted her chin, eyes flashing.

Lexi could barely get the next word out over the lump in her throat. "Or?"

Ms. Becky shrugged. "Or you can go back to the life the Imperium assigned to you. Make babies and behave yourself.

Then the Imperium might forgive you and leave both you and your father in peace."

Neither option sounded great. Though her father frustrated her to distraction, she didn't want to put him in harm's way, but someone needed to stop the Imperium and bring the right to choose back to the world. Mom would if she were here. "I'm in."

After Janie returned Lexi to the greenhouse, a message buzzed on Lexi's watch. She tapped it to read.

> *Congratulations on your wedding. We hope your union is fruitful. Rumi and I would love to have you over to our place for dinner tonight. Fresh veggies from the greenhouse will be on the menu. Bring Reeves so we can meet him.*
>   *Dad and Rumi*

Spending the evening with her father and his replacement wife had to be the ultimate betrayal of Mom's memory. Still, it sounded an awful lot better than getting the honeymoon started with Reeves. That enormous bed... She shivered.

Before she returned home, she had to see Aponi. Her friend looked so nervous at the doctor's appointment. Lexi needed to check in on her. Make sure she was okay. Something didn't feel right, and whatever it was niggled at the back of Lexi's brain.

The hallway to Aponi's apartment was vacant. Everyone would be at work or school by this time of day. Aponi and her husband would have been as well—if they weren't still on their honeymoon. Lexi scanned her palm on the security pad and announced herself.

No response.

She waited a minute and knocked. "Aponi? You home?"

The door opened, but the middle-aged woman in front of her wasn't Aponi. She wore the clothing of the maintenance crew. Dark shadows underscored her eyes. "No one's home, kiddo." She stifled a yawn. "I'm getting this apartment ready for a new couple. They move in this afternoon."

Lexi double-checked the door number. Was she on the wrong floor? "I'm sorry. Do I have the wrong place? I thought Aponi lived here. She's on her honeymoon."

The woman referred to her watch, scrolling through a list on it. "Yeah, Aponi's one name who used to be assigned to this place. They moved out yesterday."

"Why would they move *out*? They just moved *in*."

With a shrug, the woman let out a breath. "Look, kid, I don't keep track of people. I just clean and prep apartments. You know how it goes. Maybe they got pregnant and got one of those two-bedroom places. I got work to do."

The door closed in Lexi's face. There hadn't been time for them to get pregnant yet. The Imperium would never check for a baby so soon after the wedding. And after the last time she'd seen her friend… Something was very wrong.

After lunch, Lexi scanned herself back into her new home. When she entered, Reeves sat on the couch, reading on his tablet. He set it aside, frowning. "Where'd you go? I hadn't figured I'd spend the first day of our honeymoon alone. You could have at least left a message, so I wouldn't worry."

She dropped her backpack on the counter. "You never need to worry about me. I had things to do."

His frown deepened, and he stood. "We're married now. That means we need to com–*mun*–ni–cate."

The way he pronounced each syllable as if she were hard of hearing set her nerves on edge. "Look, we need to get to my father's place. They invited us for dinner. Fresh food."

He huffed out a breath. "And what if I already made plans while you were out wandering?"

That hadn't even occurred to her. Having a husband was going to take a lot of getting used to. There wouldn't be enough hours in the day if she had to check in with him all the time. "Did you?"

His lips pressed together in a flat line. "Did I what?"

Was he purposely acting obtuse? "Did you make plans? While I was out?"

With a toss, he sent his tablet flying the short distance to the couch. "No. I didn't. But that's not the point."

No. Not obtuse. Obstinate. "Then can we go?" She swept a hand toward the door.

He balled his hands and planted them on his hips.

She imagined the gears turning in his head, trying to think through his next move. Maybe she needed to take a different approach. "Please?"

He sighed, shoulders slumping, then headed to the door. "Fine."

Thirty minutes later, they feasted on baked potatoes with real butter. A sprinkle of both salt and pepper seasoned them to perfection. A hot meal was such a treat compared to the usual protein bars. Lexi could have eaten a second spud, but one for each of them had probably set her father's budget back enough.

She swallowed the last bite and wiped her mouth with a

napkin. "That was wonderful. Thank you for inviting us."

Rumi nodded but said nothing.

Dad put his fork down on his empty plate, then his hand over Rumi's. "Thank you for cooking, Rumi. You're quite the expert in the kitchen."

His loving attention to another woman twisted the knife already poking into Lexi's gut. Such signs of affection had been rare between him and Mom. Her mother had deserved better.

Lexi averted her gaze. It landed squarely on Reeves. Warmth rushed to her cheeks while a splotch of red grew on his neck. Why did her father have to act like a teenager when the actual teenagers in the room acted more like adults?

She collected her plate and Reeves's, then carried them to the sink.

Rumi jumped up and gathered the two remaining plates and joined her at the sink. "You're so sweet to clean up, but please don't bother. I've got it."

Her father rushed to the sink and turned on the faucet. He pulled Rumi into a side hug. "I'll wash tonight. You relax and get to know my daughter and Reeves."

Lexi saw red. How dare he treat this girl like a queen when he'd been almost cold with Mom? She had to force down the scream that ached to erupt. Enough was enough. "We've got to go."

Her father's lips flattened, and his eyes narrowed. "No. We need to talk."

Chapter 13

L exi ground her teeth and glared at her father. Most likely, she had as much to say to him as he did to her, but a discussion right now was *not* a good idea. They didn't need to vent in front of Reeves and Rumi. "Let's find a day that works for both of us to meet up in private for that chat."

Her father wiped his hands on a towel and laid it on the counter. "Would you two mind giving my daughter and me a moment of privacy? Perhaps a stroll to the greenhouse?"

Reeves and Rumi rushed out of the apartment, adding to Lexi's frustration. Reeves hadn't even asked if she wanted to be left alone with her father. They'd need to discuss this later.

Once they were alone, her father began. "I can tell Rumi makes you uncomfortable, but she's family now. I'd appreciate it if you'd try to be cordial with her. She doesn't seem to have much in the way of friendships."

Her actions screamed "petulant child," but that didn't stop Lexi from scowling with her arms crossed. "How is that my problem?"

He rolled his eyes. "Why do you have to be so stubborn? You're just like your mother."

The laugh burst out before she could stop it. "Good. I'm

glad I'm like Mom. Better her than you." His wince fueled her. "At least Mom wanted to change the way the Imperium works. She wanted to stop forced marriages. Not like you—marrying someone who could be your daughter, for crying out loud. What were you thinking?"

At first, he backed off as if she'd slapped him. Then he caught a second wind and went on the attack. "You think I *wanted* to marry again? You gave me no option, Lexi. I know you failed the test on purpose. You could have pleaded illness that day. Could have taken the test again." His fists clenched at his sides. "As you are perfectly aware, I don't choose the age or any other feature of the wife the Imperium assigns to me."

She stalked closer and shoved a finger into his chest. "People like you came up with this crazy plan. People like you perpetuate the control. It's slavery. I read Mom's diary. I know how you treated her when she told you she couldn't have more children."

The blood rushed out of his face, and he stumbled back a step. "You don't know the entire story. Your mother wanted to run away. To join some rebellion." He opened his palms toward her, pleading with his eyes. "But the only way to change the system was from within. All the rebels did was cause the Freedom Force to crack down even harder. We need to get enough people into power who want to change the laws. It's the only way."

His words sucked the bluster from her lungs. Breathless, she goggled at him. Was it possible he didn't agree with everything the Imperium stood for, after all? Had she been too judgmental?

"But…" Oh, how she hated how childish she sounded. "But you married Rumi before we'd even finished mourning Mom.

How could you?"

His green eyes dimmed, the energy draining from them like a plant dying. "They'd have reassigned me to the men's barracks the moment the mourning ended. Once they reassign you to the barracks, your political career is over. You're considered old and washed up. I'd have been demoted instead of promoted. My opportunity to create change would have ended." He reached out and touched her arm. "I couldn't let that happen."

She yanked away from him. The entire situation swirled in her confused brain. It was too much to digest. She needed to end this conversation and used the first available excuse. "I need to find Reeves. He shouldn't have to spend his honeymoon alone."

Lexi had no intention of finding Reeves. She needed time alone. Time to process what she'd found out. How could her parents have been in sync about changing the Imperium's laws, and yet opposites on how to accomplish the task? Couldn't they have compromised?

Back in her apartment, she awaited Reeves. It would've been more polite to wait for him at her father's place, but she couldn't. Who could endure another minute with her father lavishing attention on Rumi?

Wanting to feel close to Mom, she dug out the diary, flopped down on the couch, then opened it to the next entry.

I dread the day when Lexi will start school. If only there was any other option than sending her into the machine that is the Imperium educational system. Allowing them to mold her thoughts. Can I influence Lexi without putting her in danger? I want to tell her everything. The truth about what the Imperium is doing. Has done.

Will do.

But she's too young. I can't risk such secrets to an immature mind. I must wait until she's older. Old enough to understand when to lie and when to tell the truth. It seems so wrong to teach a child such things.

Lexi's blood went cold. Mom wanted to tell her about the Imperium—about Y. But it hadn't been safe.

But why hadn't Mom said anything when she handed the necklace over? Perhaps she'd planned to later that day. Lexi clenched her jaw. She'd give anything to sit with Mom right now and pelt her with question after question until she knew everything there was to know.

The front door clicked open, and Reeves walked in, his face expressionless. If only she could read his mind. Or better yet, if he could know how she felt without her having to tell the whole wretched story of her parents' conflict. She closed the diary.

He walked across the room and sat on the couch beside her. His eyes searched hers as if looking for the answers. "Are you okay?"

No. Not that. Anything but pity.

The tears pooled in her eyes. After gritting her teeth, she squeezed her eyes shut, willing the tears to stay put. The next word came out sounding moist, as if she'd hauled it out of an ocean of sadness. "No."

Then he did something unexpected. He pulled her into his arms and squeezed—hard. "I'm sorry about your mom. Your dad too."

The dam broke, and the tears came in torrents. Sobs rocked her body. She'd lost her entire family. Reeves rubbed her back and cradled her. "It's going to be okay. I promise."

Regaining her composure took too much time. "I'll be right back."

She dashed to the bathroom, grabbed a washcloth out of the closet, ran it under cool water, and cleaned her face. In the mirror, she saw a child, red-nosed and watery-eyed.

Quit being a baby. Woman up.

After a few deep breaths, she rinsed again in the cool water, and the red blotches began to fade. Only then did she feel composed enough to go back and talk to her husband.

He waited for her on the couch, his smile tentative. "Better?"

With a quick nod, she sat beside him. "Yes. Thank you. I don't normally fall apart like that. I guess it's been building for a while."

His eyes softened. "I could tell you were struggling. Is there anything I can do to help?"

How had she lucked out to be assigned to such an intuitive and sweet fellow? She'd been wrong to judge him before she'd even gotten to know him. "You already have. Thanks."

He stood and dug into his back pocket. "I almost forgot. It was the strangest thing. We ran into a red-haired girl in the greenhouse while Rumi and I were giving you and your dad time alone. Never met her before, but she seemed to know you and I were married and asked me to hand this to you. If Janie's a friend of yours, why wouldn't she just send a regular message?"

He handed over a folded note.

How would Janie have known about Reeves, much less recognized him? Lexi would ask the next time she visited. Unfolding the note, she gasped as shock rocketed through her at the signature—Aponi. "This came from my best friend, but

I don't understand why Janie would have it."

"Dunno." Reeves shrugged. "She said it was important, though."

Lexi's nerves tingled, and her gut clenched. First, Aponi wasn't in her apartment. Now, Janie had a note from her. This couldn't be good. Her hand shook as she read.

> *Lexi:*
>
> *When they ran my blood work, they found a damaged gene. They said I won't have normal children. They annulled my marriage, and now I'm living in the Favela. I'm so frightened. Come find me. I need to talk to you.*
> *Your BFF,*
> *Aponi*

Lexi couldn't have imagined anything worse. The Imperium hadn't simply called off the marriage. They'd abandoned Aponi to a fate no one deserved.

Her heart pounded in her ears, and when she made eye contact again with Reeves, his eyes widened. "What is it?"

She sprang to her feet. "It's Aponi. They've annulled her marriage and kicked her out of the Imperium. She's living in the Favela. I have to go to her."

Before she could speed past him, he put an arm out to stop her. "Wait. You can't storm out into the Favela. First, it isn't allowed. Second, it's late, which means it's dark outside. It's not safe."

She jerked away. "*That* is why I have to go now. She's out there alone."

"Lexi." He stopped her again with his hands on her shoulders. "Can't you see she isn't alone? She's with Janie. Right? How else did we get the note?"

Her breaths came in gulps, her heart raced, and she struggled to break his grip on her until he gave her a little shake.

"Look at me." Compassion glossed his blue eyes. "We'll figure this out together—I promise. You're exhausted. It's been a stressful day. We need to think clearly—make a plan—before we go running out into the streets."

She stared into his face, desperate to find out if he was telling the truth. Would he work with her to find Aponi? Or was he trying to stop her from going on her own?

If only she knew him better—his looks, his ethics. But everything she knew about him indicated he was kind, and he was right too, hard as that was to admit. It wouldn't be safe to run around in the Favela at night. They needed to find Janie again, and the best chance for that was during the hours the greenhouse was open.

With a shrug, she pulled away from his grasp once again. "Okay. We'll wait. But tomorrow morning, with or without you, I'm heading out to find my friend."

He blew out a breath that came across as relief and stuffed his hands into his pockets. "I can live with that."

The adrenaline rush of fear ebbed from her body, leaving her limbs like leaden weights. Exhaustion over her roller-coaster emotions caught up with her, and she dropped back onto the couch. "No way am I going to sleep tonight."

He sank beside her, putting his hand over hers. "I know what you mean."

They sat together without a word. His hand warmed her own to the point she felt the heat of it ease its way up her arm and into her body. At first, the touch brought comfort, but with each passing second, his closeness brought on unease.

Was this it? They were married. The Imperium expected children. She'd heard the whispers about men and their needs and wants.

His hand squeezed hers. Then he gave it a gentle shake. "Hey. It's okay. We barely know each other."

How could he have known what she was thinking? And yet it appeared he did. The only words that came to mind were the Imperium marriage slogan they had drummed into her head throughout school. "One marriage—many children."

He busted out laughing. Not a chuckle, but a full-belly contagious laugh. Before she knew it, she'd joined him until they were both in tears and gasping for breath.

Reeves swiped at his eyes. "Isn't the Imperium going to be oh-so disappointed when they find out we haven't consummated the marriage?"

But the words were a bucket of water thrown on her, because, suddenly, the situation wasn't funny any longer. There would be tests—exams. If they didn't find evidence they were at least trying, there would be consequences.

Every thought must have shown on her face because his smile vanished, and he put an arm around her. "That was kind of a boneheaded thing to say. Sorry."

"No." The word came out with a croak. She cleared her throat and tried again. "It's okay. You're right. They expect us to make babies. I–I just don't know if I can."

He squeezed her tight against his side. "Let's not worry about that right now. There's plenty of time to get to know each other before we worry about children. Besides, we need to find your friend. That's our first concern."

She nodded. If they were going to get to know each other, she'd have to let him in on everything. He'd seemed like such a believer in the Imperium. Could she trust him to share the secret she held about her family?

Perhaps she could start small. Since Mom was beyond hurting, she'd begin with the diary. "Let's start with a brief family history. I'll tell you about my mom. Then you can tell me about yours."

His smile was so genuine she must've made the right decision. "I'm all ears."

Chapter 14

Lexi woke to a painful ache in her neck. She reached to rub it and jumped when she brushed against another body. The dark room, combined with her bleary eyes, had her confused.

The last thing she remembered was giving her eyes a brief rest last night as they'd grown heavy with the long conversation. She sent out a hand to explore. Reeves's arm rested behind her. His breaths came out soft and rhythmic.

She was safe. At home. With her *husband*.

The thought still sounded foreign. How long would it take before her marital status sunk in?

Married. Crazy.

With a catlike stretch, she eased off the couch, careful not to wake him. He deserved extra time to rest.

They'd stayed up late last night. Or would that be early this morning? It had been well past midnight the last time she'd looked.

She padded to the bathroom and wished she'd been more upfront about her mom's potential involvement with the rebel group. His shocked look at the first disclosure of her parents' disagreements ended any further sharing. She'd have to be careful what she disclosed until she got a better sense of whether he would side with his wife or stick to the Imperium's staunch beliefs.

Stepping into the shower's warm spray, Lexi remembered his description of his siblings and home life. What would it have been like growing up with a brother or sister? It had always been just her, whereas Reeves had one of each, both older than he was.

The splendor of a four-bedroom apartment must have been amazing. His family lived the ideal life the Imperium touted as the goal for all citizens. More children equaled more wealth, as the government rewarded each birth with an upgraded lifestyle.

As she toweled off, she recalled the sad crinkle of his eyes when he described his loving parents. He'd experienced a home where his family displayed affection. She could see the pain of his parents losing their apartment now that their last child had moved out. The Imperium lavished opulence on couples producing offspring, but their benevolence ended once the children were on their own.

Some newlyweds took their parents in to avoid seeing them separated into the women's and men's barracks after they no longer had children to raise.

Guilt twinged her. She should have offered to allow his parents to live with them. It wouldn't kill her to continue sleeping on the couch. She'd done as much for years once her grandparents took her bedroom. Her lack of a close relationship with her father didn't mean she couldn't be close to Reeves's parents—eventually.

Wait. I'm married now. That means we *would have to sleep on the couch.*

Best to leave that problem for another day. Besides, his

brother or sister probably already took them in. He hadn't seemed concerned, and she hadn't asked. She'd have to at some point. Today, she had a mission—find Aponi.

She dipped her toothbrush into the brushing powder. After a few strokes, there was a tap on the door, and Reeves's voice came from the other side. "Morning. Don't mean to rush you, but you've got a visitor."

Aponi? She spit into the sink. Not likely. "Who is it?"

A voice she recognized came from further away. "Your father."

It was hard to frown and rinse, but she managed. What was *he* doing here?

She rushed into her uniform, looped her hair into a ponytail, and exited the bathroom.

Her father sat on the couch while Reeves munched his breakfast near the counter. Her father stood when she entered the room, his gaze darting between Reeves and her. "Morning."

She stuffed her hands into her pockets. Whatever reason her father would show up must have something to do with his revelation the previous evening. "What brings you here this early?"

He held up both hands, palms outward, to Reeves. "I apologize. I keep asking you to do this, but would you mind giving me a private moment with my daughter?"

This time, Reeves waited with questioning eyes. When she gave him a terse nod, he ambled toward the bathroom. "I'll take my shower then."

The moment the bathroom door closed behind Reeves, her father waved toward the couch. "Shall we sit?"

Her muscles were as tense as a freshly coiled spring. The reason for his visit wouldn't be good. "I'd rather stand. What do you need?"

He gave her his I'm-your-father stare, the one he used whenever he wanted to drive a point home. "I sense you and Reeves could still annul the marriage. If that's true, I'm here to ask you one last time. *Please*, Lexi." His eyes captured hers— pleading. "If you take the test again, you can be an engineer. We'll live together while you enjoy two more years of school, then a new husband from Administration. We can still make change happen. From within, where it's safe."

"Safe?" Her hands clenched in her pockets. "Were you referring to the kind of safety those people had at the transport station? The ones a bomb blew into bits?"

He took a step toward her, red advancing up his throat and into his cheeks. "My point, exactly. Your mother's fascination with Y didn't save her, did it? The rebels took her and your grandparents out, just like all the rest."

The words froze her in place. Was he right? Was Mom dead because of the rebels' bombs? Had Mom ever actually joined Y? If she had, why would they have allowed one of their own to be caught up in the explosion? Nothing made sense.

He moved toward her with hands outstretched. "The Imperium knows the rebels are planning more assaults. Freedom Force guards are cracking down, making arrests." A nervous twitch set off in his eye. "The Favela is under attack, and it's going to get worse. The only way to change things moving forward will be from within. The Freedom Force will ensure that."

A lump clogged her throat. She had to find Aponi. *Fast.* "I don't have time to argue with you about this. Why can't you see that all your years within Administration haven't changed anything? Mom was right. There must have been some sort of

129

mistake or misunderstanding behind her death. There's only one way to fix this."

Her father took another step toward her. His face mottled almost purple. A vein across his temple bulged. "Don't be an idiot. They'll arrest you if you join the rebels. The Freedom Force has eyes and ears everywhere. They track each student's progress and abilities and know when something's not right. A friend tipped me off. They're going to investigate why you didn't pass the engineering test. They *will* interrogate you. The only way you can be safe is to admit you blew the test and retake it. I can still get them to allow it, but your window of opportunity is closing."

"No." Her jaw clenched so tightly she had trouble getting the word out. She stepped well into his personal space, so close she could feel her breath reflected with each word. "I've closed the window, the door, and any other way back. I know the direction I'm going, and it's the opposite of yours."

He clamped his hand around her arm as his eyes bulged. The pressure would leave a bruise, but she wouldn't break eye contact or wince. Instead, she glared right back and growled. "You may leave now."

Reeves's voice interrupted. "Whoa. What's going on here?"

The pressure on her arm vanished as her father stepped back. "Nothing. I'm leaving."

Neither Lexi nor Reeves said a word until they were alone again. The only sound was her ragged breathing.

"Want to tell me what happened?" He slipped an arm around her waist. "Are you okay?"

How could she explain everything she'd learned from Mom's diary in the next five minutes? She couldn't. She freed herself from his arm and gripped his wrist. "Do you trust me?"

He squinted at her. "I guess so?"

She marched to the door, dragging him behind. "Then we need to get to the Favela. *Now*. Aponi's in danger."

The trip back to the Administration building seemed to take forever, but when they stepped into the greenhouse, Lexi still couldn't calm her heart rate. Her father had no right to tell her what to do. He hadn't earned the honor. The only people who'd deserved that privilege were dead, and she was going to find out why.

They went to the strawberry bed first, but Janie wasn't there. They searched the entire greenhouse, aisle by aisle. Still no Janie.

Lexi's nerves, already on edge from the discussion with her father, were close to the breaking point. "I hope nothing's wrong."

Reeves placed a hand on the small of her back. "I'm sure she's fine. Probably just had a new assignment today or something."

Another worker walked past, and Lexi stopped him. "We're looking for another greenhouse worker, Janie. Do you know her?"

The worker looked up from his tablet. "Yeah. She's late. Third time this month. That girl's going to end up in big trouble if she doesn't get herself straightened out."

Without waiting for a response, he strode away.

Lexi's stomach hardened to stone, and the weight of it almost slammed her to her knees. She grabbed Reeves's wrist. "We have to find her. She's our only way in."

He placed his hand on top of hers. "Let's find the maintenance entrance. If she's coming in, we'll see her there first."

Alerts went off on both their wristwatches. They scrolled to pull up the message. Another bomb had gone off. This time, at the Administration's school for boys. Thankfully, rebels had detonated it before classes had begun. Though the school canceled lessons until further notice, the bomb hadn't killed anyone. *This time.*

Reeves's eyes narrowed. "Maybe today isn't the best day to go into the Favela."

She yanked her hand away from him. "I understand. You go ahead to the apartment. I'll be back as soon as I can."

His lips twisted into a no-nonsense line. "Um. That would be a definite no. Negatory. Not going to happen. I'm not leaving you to rush out there by yourself."

A door behind them opened, and Janie scurried through it. Lexi hissed under her breath the moment she got close enough. "Where have you been? We've been looking for you."

Janie huffed. "Busy."

When she nodded to Reeves, he returned the gesture.

Lexi wanted to jump out of her skin with frustration. "I need to see Aponi. *Now.*"

Janie addressed Lexi with a smirk, arms crossed. "You could be a bit more polite, you know. It isn't as if *I* was the one who helped her get a message to you or anything. Right?"

Ultimately, Janie was in control. There was only one way for them to get to the Favela.

Taking in a deep, calming breath, Lexi released it along with some of the tension that had been building all morning. "I'm sorry. You're right." She copped a humble stance. "Please. Could you take me to see her?"

"Thank you." Janie rubbed Lexi's shoulder. "Let me make my appearance, get a couple of things done so folks know I was here. Then we can sneak out."

Without thinking, she growled. "How long is that going to

take?"

Janie returned the snarl and got deep into Lexi's personal space, eye to eye and toe to toe. "As long as it takes to get it done. If you've got a problem with that, you'll have to find another way down."

Lexi wanted to smash something. To scream. To lash out. Something. *Anything.*

Reeves shoved an arm between them, putting space between them. He took Lexi's hand in his and pulled her behind him. "How can we help?"

All Lexi could see was Reeves's back until Janie popped her head around him to give her a sickly sweet smile. "What a gentleman. You're so kind to offer. Let me give you a list."

They spent the next hour picking strawberries and spinach while Janie ran around doing other chores. Working among the plants soothed Lexi's frustration. Her breathing returned to normal, and her hands had stopped shaking by the time Janie returned.

"Thanks for the help." Janie hauled the last crate of green leaves onto the transport cart and entered the command for it to return to the store. "Now that I'm caught up on the tasks for the day, we can leave with no one trying to hunt me down."

Finally. The hope of seeing Aponi wobbled Lexi's knees. "Let's go."

Janie led the way to the maintenance door.

Before Lexi followed Janie through it, she removed her watch. "We need to leave these here, so they can't track us into the Favela."

Reeves placed his with hers behind the giant plant.

They hurried down the maze of stairwells and hallways until they stood out in the Favela once again.

The acrid scent of smoldering chemicals clogged the air. They'd probably run out of wood and started on other materials in their heating barrels. His gaze darted from building to building as if he knew an enemy lurked in one of them.

They scurried through the streets, hugging the buildings and peering around corners. Several times, they dodged into alcoves when Freedom Force vehicles drove by. They didn't encounter anyone on the streets. Little wonder after the latest attack. The Imperium had to find someone to blame and punish. Nothing less would satisfy them.

Janie led them into a structure more like a shell than a building. It must've been a bomb victim during the war. Black scorched the cinder block walls, and the charred remains of office furniture lurked throughout the rooms they passed by.

The stairwell door hung on the top hinge, forcing them to walk sideways past it. Lexi clung to the handrail as they ascended. Fire had left holes in walls, and steps had crumbled. Reeves followed her close enough to touch her back when she hesitated at a gap. His warm hand reassured her.

On the third floor, sunlight shone through a breach in the ceiling.

Janie stopped and tapped on a door three times. When it opened, an enormous man filled the doorway. Fletcher. He grumbled. "'Bout time." Then he jerked a thumb to Reeves. "What's he doing here? I don't recall clearing a second visitor."

A woman's voice called from inside the room. "Quit being a grouch and let them in."

He shifted sideways to allow them through, shutting the door behind them. Flames that had eaten at the rest of the building had spared this room. Dust floated in the air over the dumpy furniture stacked against the walls.

As they entered, Aponi leaped off an overstuffed plaid couch and ran to Lexi, wrapping her in a fierce hug. "You came for me. I *knew* you would."

Chapter 15

Air whooshed out of Lexi's lungs as Aponi squeezed her, almost knocking her to the ground. "Whoa, I'm here. It's going to be okay."

When they parted, Aponi's eyes were red, and tears wet her cheeks. "It's been horrible. I don't know what I'd have done if Janie hadn't brought me to Ms. Becky." She hugged her arms around her middle as if to comfort herself.

Ms. Becky gripped Aponi's shoulder, then Lexi's. She nodded to Reeves, who hovered behind Lexi, just inside the door. "I see you've brought a guest."

Lexi'd forgotten her manners. "This is Reeves, my husband."

Reeves cleared his throat and thrust a hand toward Ms. Becky.

Fletcher blocked the move, placing himself between Reeves and the older woman. "We don't know whose side you're on. I don't trust as easily as Ms. Becky."

Raising his hands above his head, Reeves backed away and leaned against the doorpost. "I'm just along for the ride."

Ms. Becky huffed. "I'm sure anyone connected with our dear Lexi isn't going to turn us in. Correct, Reeves?"

He shoved his hands into his pockets. "Correct, ma'am."

Reeves. Lexi should've left him behind. That or shared more of what she knew about Mom so far. Too late now. Eventually, she needed to know if he'd support her and her family's secrets.

So many questions. She wanted to ask them all at once, but she settled on the most important one. "First, thank you for taking care of my best friend. I appreciate that."

Aponi swiped more tears from her face.

Lexi's heart ached for her friend's lost dreams. "Now that I know Aponi is safe, I need to know the truth about my mom. Was she a member of Y?"

With a huff, Ms. Becky returned to her perch on the couch, settling near its missing arm. "I explained before. The story was your mother's to tell. Not mine."

Lexi closed her eyes and sucked in a calming breath. "Yes, ma'am. But she isn't available to answer my questions now, is she?" She fixed her gaze on Ms. Becky. "Y set the bomb that killed her. Didn't they?"

Ms. Becky's lips flattened into a thin line. "Did you know your grandmother and I were best friends? We were in the same class in school. Both got married off on the same day. Both disappointed in how our 'perfect matches' worked out."

Nana—the necklace had been Nana's before it had been Mom's. "Are you trying to tell me Nana was a member of Y, not Mom?"

Ms. Becky's lips slid upward, and she patted the seat beside her. "Your nana was a spitfire. Did you know that? She turned your grandfather's behavior around to her liking, then convinced me to take on the Imperium." She traced circles in the air, capturing the essence of their surroundings. "This was her idea. Free the slaves, so to speak."

Now they were getting somewhere. Lexi ambled over to the couch and joined Ms. Becky. "What slaves? I don't understand."

Ms. Becky put a hand over Lexi's. "Anytime you force your decisions onto someone else, stealing their right to choose, you enslave them. Over time, little by little, the Imperium stole our choices. Where to work, who to marry, how many children to have, or even whether to have any—were all taken away. Your nana wouldn't have any of it." She huffed out a laugh. "Things changed a bit when she got pregnant with your mother. At first, she was angry. She'd refused to procreate to spite the Imperium. Lucky for her, your grandfather didn't turn her in for 'reeducation.' He couldn't get past her beauty or her rebellious attitude. She changed him, and they fell in love. When your mother came along, their bond grew even stronger."

Her grandparents' love had been obvious, especially in contrast to her parents' tense relationship. "Was Nana still a member when she died? Did she introduce Mom to the rebels?"

"Your grandmother and your mom didn't agree on how to raise you. They argued in this very room, many times, about when to tell you about Y." She looked at Reeves. "Son, you may want to leave the room. You can't unhear what I'm about to share with your wife. Once you know, your life will be as much in danger as hers. If you're going to bow out, now's the moment."

Reeves ducked his head, drew an invisible line on the floor with his toe, then faced the couch as he stepped across that line. "I support Lexi. No matter what."

Lexi's heart performed a flip in her chest. How had he become so devoted in such a short time? She could learn from him. "Thank you." She held up both hands to Ms. Becky.

"Tell me. *Please.*"

Ms. Becky nodded, and her well-lined brow furrowed into deeper creases before she began. "We tried to convince others first. Meetings with government officials. Rallies to end forced marriages. Protests to allow people to choose their careers." She scrubbed her hands together. "None of it worked. Those in power just tightened the reins of control."

Who could imagine the Imperium any less controlling than they were now?

Tears filled Ms. Becky's eyes. "A faction broke off from Y— those who'd run out of patience with the Imperium. They set off the first bomb, starting the next war. A fight that continues to this day, though the Imperium denies its existence."

Uncertain she wanted to know the answer, Lexi wouldn't let fear keep her from asking. "Was Nana part of the faction?"

The glassy glow receded from Ms. Becky's eyes. "No. Absolutely not." She patted Lexi's hand. "Your grandmother wanted freedom, but never at the cost of someone else's life. She was a pacifist through and through."

The irony of it wasn't lost on Lexi. "Nana started the movement that ended her life."

"Looks that way." Ms. Becky stood and brushed off the seat of her pants, perhaps mentally brushing off the thought. "But what you're asking is what *you* should do now. Isn't it?"

Lexi's body sagged. This is what she needed, though she hadn't known it. "I guess it is. I'm lost, trying to find a way to connect with Mom and Nana. Join in where they left off—if that makes sense."

Ms. Becky walked over to Reeves. "Do you understand what your wife is about to do? Once she starts down this path, there is no turning back. She'll be in the crosshairs of the Freedom

Force, and you along with her. Once they find out what she's up to, you'd both end up living on the run, as I do, if they didn't catch you first."

Something intense flashed in Reeves's eyes, but Lexi couldn't decipher their message. He rubbed his temples. "Lexi and I need to talk. Privately."

Ms. Becky chuckled. "I figured you'd be the sensible one."

A shout from the street below shot through an open window. Fletcher's spine stiffened. "Time's up, Ms. Becky. We gotta go."

Reeves closed the gap between him and Lexi in three long strides and clamped his hand around her wrist. "We're leaving. Now."

"No. Not without Aponi." She pulled back. "And we have to stay with Ms. Becky. I need to know everything."

Fletcher had already exited the room and waited in the hallway.

Ms. Becky hustled Aponi out. "You can't take your friend back inside. Neither you nor she would be safe if she were found there. That's not how to work things. Have your talk first, Lexi. You know how to find us. I'll get our connections on the inside to give you access to the Favela. When you're ready, come see me."

Aponi broke free long enough to hug Lexi. "I love you." Before they released each other, Aponi whispered in Lexi's ear. "Even my parents didn't come for me, but *you* did. Don't worry. I'll be all right with Ms. Becky now."

Then they were gone, disappearing out the door as the alarm drew closer and Aponi followed.

When Reeves and Lexi exited the room, Janie still waited, alone, at the top of the stairs. "Figured I'd better get you back to the Administration building. Wouldn't want you getting lost down here."

They dashed down alleys, once more hugging the edges and slipping into alcoves as Freedom Force members patrolled the streets. Reeves didn't let go of Lexi's wrist until they were once again safe inside, away from the Favela and the Freedom Force patrols.

They made their way back toward the Reclamation buildings, seeking the safety of their apartment. Lexi's skin crawled with every glance directed their way, as if everyone knew where they'd been—and with whom.

While they waited in the transportation hub, she recalled the last time she'd seen her loved ones. Who knew if today would be her last day alive? No one could know how much time they had left.

Once they were secure inside their apartment, Reeves blew out a long breath, as if he'd been holding it the entire return trek. He turned her to face him, his lips pressed into a thin line. "Thanks for the advanced warning. You could've told me the truth about your mom and your grandparents."

Heat rushed to her cheeks. He was right. He deserved to know everything she did. "I found my mom's diary after she died in the explosion. I knew she was involved in Y. Nana too. But I still don't know the extent of it."

His hands flew to his hips. "Where's the diary now?"

His glare had her on edge. He'd seemed so sincere in his support of Ms. Becky. This look left her wondering. Could she trust him now that he could see the potential danger? Did he want the diary to destroy it? She couldn't allow that. She hadn't even finished reading it. Life had been so busy since she'd discovered it. "It's safe."

With a huff, he drew her into an embrace and crushed her against his chest. "I'm worried about you. Can't you see that? I won't do anything to the diary. I just want us to read it all. To know every secret it holds." He pushed her back to arm's length and stared into her eyes. "Let's finish it together. Okay?"

This was it. Time to decide. Did she trust him?

His eyes implored—*trust me.*

She squirmed out of his arms, went to her backpack, and dug through it. "Come on." Moving to the couch, she sat and patted the cushion beside her. "I'll give you the highlights. Then we'll read the rest out loud."

He joined her, wrapping an arm around her shoulders.

The short version of what she'd read didn't take long. Reeves didn't appear shocked, but he'd heard a lot from Ms. Becky's revelations.

Lexi opened the diary to where she'd left off, and they bowed their heads over the next entry.

Mom came to visit today. I hate that I was crying when she got here. Gunner and I fought about Lexi— again—like always. She's showing amazing abilities for Administration work. She'd qualify for special grooming for leadership. I want him to get one of his friends to alter her record. He's got the connections and could do it. I don't want my baby to be sucked into the machine that is the Imperium. Gunner refuses. Said she's our best chance to change things from within. I'm afraid. She might change the Imperium, but with their grooming process, it's more likely they'd change her. Forever.

A knock at their door sent a chill through Lexi. The interruption's timing as she learned about the Imperium's plan to brainwash her set her teeth on edge. *You're being ridiculous.* The Freedom Force wasn't about to barge in and drag her off for additional "education."

Reeves rose. "I'll get it."

Lexi's heart pounded as she slipped the diary back into its hiding place, then put the backpack behind the couch. She waited, hands clenched at her sides, watching her husband's movements.

His body blocked her view of the hallway when he opened the door. "What a surprise. Come on in."

Rumi stepped through the doorway and smiled at Lexi as they made eye contact. "I hope I'm not interrupting. Your father insisted I come by."

Now, *why* would her father send Rumi to talk to her? Did he think Rumi would have any greater influence on Lexi's decisions? "Why didn't he come himself?"

Reeves closed the door behind their guest and offered her a seat at the table. "Can I get you a glass of water or anything?"

"No th–thank you." Rumi dipped her head and swallowed at the quaver in her voice. When she raised her chin, she reached toward Lexi as if she could breach the emotional space between them. "Lexi, your father's boss summoned him to an urgent meeting. He wouldn't tell me what it was about, only that I should come here and warn you to stay away from the Favela."

An icy chill rushed through Lexi's veins. "What makes him think I'd go there?"

Rumi's spurned hand shook. She moved it into her lap. Something had frightened her. "He said he couldn't tell me more, but I was to tell you it wasn't safe. Said I should come here, warn you to stay home. He also said I shouldn't come back to the apartment until he messaged me."

A tear slipped from Rumi's eye, and she swiped it away.

Reeves went to the kitchen, retrieved a glass, filled it with water, and set it in front of Rumi. "I'll grab you something for your nose. One second."

When he passed by Lexi, he gave her a look, then twitched his head toward Rumi. The message couldn't have been clearer. *Help her.*

Why should I? Rumi didn't deserve her support. She tried to replace Mom. Lexi's stomach knotted. *That's not true.* Her father had acted, not Rumi. She was just the pawn in the Imperium's game of control.

Lexi huffed out a breath and joined Rumi at the table, patting her on the shoulder before claiming the chair beside her. "He gets called into important meetings all the time. His job in security is hush-hush, though. You'll get used to it."

Rumi shook her head, then sipped her water. "He looked worried. The way he told me to warn you scared me. Something's not right."

Reeves walked into the room with a washcloth when all their watch alarms went off.

National broadcast begins in five minutes. Required viewing for all citizens.

A shiver ran down Lexi's spine. Such announcements were rare and reinforced Imperium messages. They all moved to the couch as their vis unit dropped from the ceiling and lit up.

As the national anthem played, the four mottos of the Imperium scrolled across the screen.

Unity above all else.

Hard work lifts us all.

A young Imperium is a thriving Imperium.

One marriage—many children.

Then the national spokesperson, Tempest Malachy, with her long blond hair and heart-shaped face, came into view. Her frown stressed the announcement's serious nature. "Citizens of the Imperium, once again, rebels have struck against our collective union, trying to weaken us—divide us." The inset frame displayed the national flag, then a video feed of the Favela. "Our citizens need not be concerned. The Imperium is unshakable. Our Freedom Force will prevail. Even as I speak, they are carrying out their mission to rid our nation of those who would strike at our very soul."

In the background inset, vagrants from the Favela were being rounded up and beaten in front of the cameras. They Tasered one man who tried to run. He lay on the ground, convulsing.

A single thought raced through Lexi's mind, emerging from her mouth in a yelp. "Aponi!

Chapter 16

Lexi's lungs seized and refused to pull in another breath. Her words came out choked as she dashed toward the door. "We have to go back. Aponi isn't safe."

Reeves beat Lexi to the exit and blocked her way. "We're not going anywhere. Your father and Rumi warned us, and we're going to heed that warning and wait right here until he gives the all clear."

Lexi tried to weave around him, dodging one arm as it attempted to capture hers but failing to escape the second. He was like an impenetrable fortress. "No. We can't leave her."

He placed a palm on her cheek, forcing her to make eye contact. "Calm. Down."

After another yank of her arm, she realized his hold wouldn't release until he chose to do so. For now, that fortress held her back, penned her in. An angry tear escaped, and she growled. "I'll calm down as soon as you let me go."

The wag of his head reinforced his message. "Not going to happen. Let's have a seat and talk through this."

Rumi's face came into view, and her wide eyes begged Lexi to stop. "I trust your father, Lexi. You must know he loves you and wants to keep you safe. Something big is happening. We need to do what he says and stay inside."

Resistance wouldn't work. Reeves was too strong. Sometimes it stunk to be female. Lexi turned away from the door. He released her to stomp into the living room and flounce onto the couch. Then he sat beside her and, with a solid hold, entwined his fingers with hers, though she resisted.

With his free hand, he gestured for Rumi to join them. "There's room on the couch or you can bring a kitchen chair over. We need to talk through our options."

Talk through options? They needed action—not talk.

The newscast droned on about the criminals the Freedom Force was rounding up. Tempest read a list of those arrested— names Lexi didn't recognize. Then she ticked off the crimes the Imperium had levied against them.

Insurrection. Terrorist threats. Murder. An endless list.

Faces flashed across the screen as the drone cams documented the Freedom Force's purge. No sign of Ms. Becky, Fletcher, or Janie. Most likely, they had experience with avoidance tactics. They'd kept Aponi safe. Yet Lexi's heart ached at the abuse heaped onto the poor, starved people the Freedom Force had captured.

She couldn't take it anymore. It wasn't fair to punish the homeless for the terrorist group's actions. Their bedraggled faces didn't exude rebellion, but rather defeat and hopelessness. They had the wrong people.

Reeves sucked in a sudden breath and squeezed Lexi's arm. What had she missed? She scanned the screen, searching. Her gaze landed on Aponi's terrified face, and her heart jumped into her throat. *No!*

On the video screen, Aponi struggled against the Freedom Force officer as he scanned her palm for identification. The struggle was no contest. The moment he'd scanned her, his

147

hulking arms twisted hers behind her back, zip-tied them, then tossed her into the back of a van as if she were a bag of trash.

I have to save her. Lexi popped off the couch, but her legs refused to cooperate. As if her muscles had jellified, she crumpled to her knees.

Now that the Imperium had Aponi's name, Tempest read it to the audience as she continued to tick off names of the captured. "Aponi Liam. The Imperium has detained Aponi Liam as a person of interest in the recent transportation hub bombing. That assault on our city resulted in the deaths of hundreds of Imperium citizens. What a relief to have such an insidious criminal off the streets."

Lexi couldn't breathe. They'd accused Aponi of the bombing that killed Mom? Anyone who knew Aponi wouldn't believe such nonsense.

The television cut to a scene of a reporter interviewing an Imperium citizen in a white Administration uniform. The male reporter with curly dark hair focused on the young woman. "What are your thoughts on today's delinquent roundup?"

The woman spoke into the camera with a hand over her heart as if sharing with her best friend. "I can't tell you how relieved I am that they've arrested so many dangerous criminals. I'll sleep sound tonight knowing we're all safer because of this campaign."

The camera flashed to another scene of the high council seated around an oval wooden table.

Ms. Malachy's voice spoke while the camera panned each council member. "Though the council's spokesperson in-dicated this wave of arrests is only the beginning, most citizens we've polled gave high marks for their brave actions to preserve our city's unity."

Tempest's face once again filled the screen. "Signing off for today."

Her image dissolved, and the four mottos scrolled lazily across the screen.

Unity above all else.

Hard work lifts us all.

A young Imperium is a thriving Imperium.

One marriage—many children.

The screen went black.

Lexi's body wouldn't respond to her demand to stand. To take action and save her friend. Instead, she remained heaped on the floor as if gravity had sucked her into its center, refusing to let her go.

Sobs nearby caught her attention. Rumi had buried her face in the washcloth. Her shoulders quaked.

Reeves sat on the couch, unmoving, face red with a frown as deep as a bottomless pit.

The sight struck a nerve and helped Lexi find the resolve she'd forgotten. Adrenaline surged through her body, giving her legs the strength they'd lost.

Ready to act, she stood, snagged his arm, and yanked him off the couch. She hoped the fierce look in his eyes reflected her own.

Her free hand pulled the washcloth away from Rumi. Rumi's red eyes met hers and widened as if in shock at what they saw in Lexi's. Rumi sucked in a breath, then stood beside them, and accepted Lexi's proffered hand.

Lexi squeezed their fingers. "We're not going to let the Imperium have the last word on this. I'm here for each of you if you need me, but I'm going to fight for those people who are being rounded up for crimes we know they didn't commit."

Rumi shook her head. "You can't fight the Imperium. There's no way."

At a knock, Lexi and Reeves made eye contact. Then she stepped forward to answer the door.

Reeves held her back. "No. Let me."

She refused to release his hand. "Together."

They walked to the door and looked at the camera. Her father stood there, his head swiveled from side to side as if looking for pursuers. Reeves opened the door, and her father darted into the apartment and shut the door behind him.

His frantic eyes searched the room until they landed on Rumi. The moment he saw her, he put a hand to his heart and breathed out a sigh. "You're all here."

He caught Lexi in a bone-crushing embrace. Then Rumi joined them. "I've been frantic you hadn't gotten my message." He released Lexi, then faced Reeves, not fully releasing Rumi. "Thank you for keeping Rumi safe."

Lexi stiffened her spine. Her father could use his connections to help her friend. "They took Aponi. Why would they do that? She couldn't have had anything to do with the bomb. We have to get her out of jail."

"No." His eyes flashed. "We're doing no such thing. You need to stay put and keep out of this." He released Rumi, leveling his full attention on Lexi. "You're not getting the point here, kiddo. *Nobody* can do *anything* for your friend now. You need to keep yourself out of trouble—like, by retaking your test and getting reassigned to Administration. Two more years of protection in the school for engineering. We might even get you into a leadership role."

He then clamped a hand on Reeves's shoulder. "Nothing personal. But my daughter's poor decisions will drag you in, eventually. You're safer without her."

Reeves's eyebrows shot up. "Excuse me?" He snugged Lexi to his side. "Your daughter is onto something important. You should want to support her instead of ordering her around like a child."

She blinked. *Did I hear that right?* Reeves had taken her side against her father. Most people would fear repercussions if they offended someone with her father's political clout. But not her man. A warmth swelled in her belly.

Unable to hold back a grin, she clasped Reeves's hand, and together, they faced her father. "I think it's time for you to take Rumi home. She's had a rough night."

He frowned. "Lexi, I—"

"Good night, Mr. Verity." Reeves's interruption left her father's mouth gaping and Lexi's heart lighter than air.

Inappropriate, yes, but she couldn't stop smiling as her father dragged Rumi to the door. Right before they disappeared through it, Rumi mouthed, "Thank you."

Lexi gave her a terse nod. Her father was blind to the truth, and he'd pollute the thoughts of his new, gullible wife in time. She couldn't help but feel sorry for Rumi getting stuck with a man like her father.

Once the door closed behind their visitors, Lexi hugged Reeves, squeezing as hard as she could muster. "Thank you for supporting me."

He returned the embrace. "We've got this. Together."

Her cheeks warmed under his gaze as they separated. His smile sent butterflies aflutter in her stomach. *Time for a change of subject. Now.* "We need a plan. How can we save Aponi?"

The sparkle in his eyes dimmed. "I hate to say it, but I may be on your father's side on this issue. I don't see what we could do for her. Anything we try would paint a target on our foreheads. The Imperium's Freedom Force would be on us like shadows."

And here I thought he was on my side. "You want to leave her there? In jail?"

He jammed his hands into his pockets, and his glare zeroed in on her. "Of course, I don't *want* to abandon her. What choice do we have?"

Every butterfly that had occupied her stomach fled. A slow burn replaced them. "We can find Ms. Becky and Fletcher. They'll have a plan—they must. If they don't, we need to convince them to make one."

"Ha. Good one." His face twisted into a grimace. "You don't get it. *Think*, Lexi. The Freedom Force is rounding up everybody they find in the Favela. If Ms. Becky isn't already on one of those buses dragging people to lockdown, then she's going to be deep into a hideaway."

He's a quitter. The urge to scream floated closer to the surface with each word he said. "We have to try." She stalked toward the door. "*I* have to try."

The speed with which his arm snaked out and grabbed hers shocked her. She yanked—hard. "Let me go."

He didn't release her. Instead, he placed his body between hers and the door. "No."

"You can't keep me here." She tried to overcome his strength, but it didn't take an engineer's brain to realize she couldn't. "I'm your wife, not your slave."

He closed his eyes, sucked in a deep breath, then blew it out, slow and steady. "I know that. But you aren't thinking straight. Calm down. Let's get past tonight and see what things look like in the morning."

Her anger morphed, and frustration left her itching to do something. Anything. "*Things* are going to look like my friend is still in jail in the morning. What else would there be to see?"

His eyes softened, and his tone gentled. "Lexi. *Please*. I promise we'll do something. *Tomorrow*." The grip on her arm loosened, then released. "I'm in this with you, but we have to be smart about it. Rushing out there is going to get us into the same spot as Aponi. That won't help her."

Just great. He was right.

The tension inside her had built to demand release. She screamed out a curse and kicked a chair over, then hopped up and down on one foot, gasping for the toe she may have just broken.

Reeves's laughter burst out.

She glared.

He held a hand to her the moment she stopped bouncing, and she accepted it. "Come on. We need to get some rest if we're going to be ready to think of fresh ideas in the morning." He led her to the bedroom, opened the door, and ushered her in. "You can have the bed. I'll take the couch."

The king-sized mattress made her realize what a long day it had been. Exhaustion pulled at her body, even as she noticed his droopy eyes. He hadn't gotten any more sleep last night than she had. "No. It's okay. I'm used to sleeping on the pullout."

He nodded, but he still held her hand. "You know. We *are* married. You're welcome to sleep with me in the big comfy bed."

Tempting. It would be so nice not to be alone tonight. But then again, she'd slept alone her entire life. It would feel weird

153

to have someone in her space. Then she remembered the ache in her neck she'd woken with this morning after sleeping on his arm on the couch. "Maybe another night? I'm not ready."

He gave her a sweet smile. "I understand. I'll leave the bedroom door open, though, in case you change your mind."

If her world weren't such a tangled mess right now, she'd follow him anywhere, including into that bed. But for now, she needed a good night's rest. They had to find solutions. Tomorrow.

Chapter 17

L exi bolted out of bed and her night terror with the sting of her watch's missed-alarm shock. Her hand slapped at the offending wristband, acknowledging her status.

"I'm awake already."

Though the groggy sensation disoriented her, at least the premature exit from sleep rescued her. Remnants of the nightmare hovered like a dark cloud, and she shivered.

She'd been the only one left alive among piles of dead bodies. The bloodied faces of Reeves, Aponi, and every member of the rebel group had lain around her, staring through unseeing eyes. Remembering Rumi's body lying atop Dad's prone corpse almost made Lexi want to go see them—to ensure they were alive and well. Almost.

When would her father realize she'd chosen her path? Just as he'd selected his own. Did the dream reveal some deep-seated fear that their paths would conflict some day? Another shudder ran through her.

Her watch buzzed and flashed. Another message from the Imperium.

Required viewing for all Imperium citizens in fifteen minutes. Please find your closest vis unit.

Now what? She hefted her tired body off the couch and started fixing the covers to slide the bed back into the couch.

"Morning." Reeves exited the bathroom door, slicked-back hair still wet from the shower. "Hope I didn't wake you when I got up."

His smile drew her in. Impossible not to respond. Her lips twitched upward. "Not even close. I ended up with the morning snap because I missed the alarm."

Huffing out a laugh, he wandered over. "Here, let me help."

Though she'd put her own bed away for as long as she could remember, she appreciated his help, his attention. After the disturbing images now imprinted on her mind, she wanted to be near him. To feel the security of another human, alive and warm, next to her. His warmth dispelled the lingering visions.

They'd plopped the last cushion into place, morphing her bed into a couch when the vis unit turned on to depict Tempest Malachy's somber visage. The four mottos of the Imperium made their way across the monitor. Tempest wouldn't dare begin before the last period of the final motto had displayed.

Unity above all else.

Reeves sat on the couch and grasped Lexi's hand, hauling her down beside him. As his powerful arm enveloped her shoulders, she nestled closer to his side, seeking solace in his presence. With each breath, the intoxicating earthy aroma of herbs clinging to him transported her to a realm where nature's essence intertwined them.

Hard work lifts us all.

He was alive and warm, and he smelled amazing. She allowed herself just to be while they waited for Tempest.

A young Imperium is a thriving Imperium.

Could Reeves derive comfort from her presence as much as

156

she did from his? One of these days, she needed to woman up and discuss their future. But not today. Today, she just wanted to exist with him.

One marriage—many children.

The last word trailed away, and Tempest cleared her throat. "I have solemn news to share with our viewers."

Another video overlaid the newscaster in the top-right corner. Snippets of the previous evening's raid on the Favela played as a reminder of what had occurred. As if Lexi could ever get the scenes out of her head.

She squeezed in tight against Reeves, uncertain whether she wanted comfort or to siphon strength from him to follow through. She needed to act today. Free Aponi—somehow.

Reeves stiffened as the image switched to an Imperium courtroom where prisoners stood before a judge in a single-file line. Tempest's voice spoke over the courtroom proceedings. "Overnight, the efficiency of the Imperium's court system provided the required speedy trial for those rounded up in yesterday's raid of the Favela. Those accused of crimes against our great city stood trial with representation provided."

A lawyer attended to the first person in line while the judge spoke, then listened to the accused's representative, then spoke again. The judge's gavel smacked hard against the round wooden base. Though they couldn't hear the word spoken, large red letters flashed on the screen across the bottom of the display—*G-U-I-L-T-Y.*

Even without hearing the gavel's crack, Lexi jumped at the decree. Guards dragged the first person in line away as the next person stepped up beside the same lawyer, and the process repeated itself. Smack. Guilty. Next.

The line spread out, too long for the camera to take it all in.

Lexi moved closer to the vis, kneeling at its base, one hand reaching to touch the smooth screen. So many people. Was Aponi in the line?

This farce wasn't justice. She fought to breathe past the weight in her chest. "They can't do that. Can they?"

Reeves moved to join her feet from the vis screen. "I wouldn't have thought so if you'd have asked me a month ago. But there doesn't seem to be anyone to stop them, does there?"

Her breathing had become more labored. Her heart pumped as if she'd been sprinting up the stairwells in the maintenance areas. "We need to do something."

With a huff, he dragged a hand through his wet locks. "I'm with you. But what can we do? We can't storm into the courtroom and say, 'Hey, no fair. Cut it out.'"

How right he was. And how she hated that. They needed not only a plan but also supporters. Lots of them. Her father would be no help. All he'd parrot back if she asked for advice would be for her to retake the stupid test.

In this moment, she wanted to blow up the test. Blow up the school. Blow up the Imperium. With each hammer of the gavel, the determination to join the rebellion grew stronger.

The scene on the vis switched to a prison yard. Tempest's voice walked them through what they were about to witness. "Along with the required trial, the Imperium will waste no time to bring those convicted to swift justice. All the Imperium will sleep sounder tonight, knowing our loved ones are safe from terrorists."

Lexi sucked in a breath. The cameras weren't panning across a prison yard. Lines of detainees stood chained together in rows of ten. A guard yanked the shackles of the prisoner closest to him, and the rest chained to him followed. They lined up in front of a thick wooden wall covered in pockmarks.

Shivers iced her blood. "No. They can't."

Reeves grabbed her arm and tried to turn her away from the video feed, but the Imperium gave him no time. The roar of gunfire exploded out of the vis as if the newscast producer amplified the noise for effect.

The row of prisoners toppled.

A Freedom Force van appeared on the screen, backing up to the lifeless bodies. A guard pulled a chain from the back of the van and clamped it to the manacles of the man who'd fallen first in the lineup. As the vehicle hauled the line of bodies out of sight, they escorted another line of prisoners in.

The first woman in this new lineup struggled against the guard, fighting with all her might to keep herself and those behind her away from the firing squad. Another guard soon joined in, slapped the woman hard across the face, then yanked in unison with the first guard.

After a beat, Lexi jolted. The entire row of ten was all female. The tiniest person trailing behind had a familiar gait. Springing to her feet, Lexi screamed. "Aponi."

This time, Reeves jumped between Lexi and the vis screen. His hands held her face as tears flowed hot and fast down her cheeks. "Don't look, Lexi. Look at me. Eyes on me."

She struggled to get away. She needed out of the apartment. She needed to go to her friend. "No. They *can't*. We have to do something."

In response, Reeves secured her into a tight embrace and clamped his hands over her ears to shield her from the inevitable. But his palms couldn't mask the amplified gunfire, and the explosive barrage of bullets dropped her to her knees, sobbing.

She didn't know how long she cried, but he kneeled beside her, holding her until she ran dry. It took even longer after that before she could speak. "I doubt they'll allow proper funerals."

He stood, drawing her off the floor and onto the couch. "Probably not."

The vis had gone silent. She wanted to tear it into pieces with her bare hands so it could never show another such charade.

Every inch of her ached. Last night's nightmare coming true. She looked Reeves in the eyes. They were somber but dry. The concern in them caused her own to water again.

"Excuse me for a minute." With a pat on his arm, she extricated herself from his hold and went to the bathroom. A glance in the mirror revealed swollen eyes and blotchy red skin. *Nice.*

"Pull yourself together." She pointed a finger at the sad girl staring at her from the mirror. "You are the only person who can keep Aponi's death from being meaningless."

She growled, deep in her throat, and those eyes morphed into angry, fierce orbs, ready for action. The woman in the reflection had no more time for tears or sorrow.

After washing her face in cool water, she stole extra moments to collect herself. Another glance in the glass proved she was ready to rejoin Reeves.

When she came out of the bathroom, he was already standing as if he knew she'd be ready to leave at a moment's notice. He'd crossed his arms over his chest, his stare vacant, his mind elsewhere.

She stepped up beside him. "I need to tell you something, and I need you to hear me. Truly *hear* me."

He nodded as he uncrossed his arms.

She continued. "I'm going back to the Favela. It might be

me on the vis tomorrow, following in Aponi's footsteps. But I'm beyond caring."

He opened his mouth, but she held up a finger before he could get the first word out. "I'm not done yet."

After sucking his lips into his mouth as if to swallow back the words he'd prepared, he blinked.

She'd take that as acceptance. "I already know what you're going to say, but I don't want you to come with me."

"No way—"

She stabbed her upheld finger high, and he closed his mouth again. "You still have a family. All that's left of mine is a father who cares more about his career than why someone blew his wife and in-laws into tiny bits."

"What am I then?" He cut her off, his eyes crinkled as if she'd caused him pain. "I thought I meant *something* to you. Have I been kidding myself?"

What a klutz she'd been. She wanted to keep him safe, not stab him in the heart. Her own heart ached at the sight. "I'm not good at the whole romance thing." Reaching out, she put a hand on his arm, dragged it down until it reached his hand, then entangled her fingers with his. "You need to know I don't expect you to come with me. I'm almost positive I'll be dead tomorrow. You don't deserve that."

His lips twisted sideways. "My mama warned me that someday someone I loved would break my heart. She said *that* was when I needed to lean in, dig deeper, and be broken together. It's the only way a marriage can work." He squeezed her hand, brought it up to his lips, and kissed it. "You're not getting rid of me that easy. We're in this together. All the way."

She wanted to laugh. Would have, if what they had agreed to weren't a death sentence. "Together then. It's time to go

back to the Favela."
Until death do us part.

Chapter 18

Lexi and Reeves made their way down the empty hallways. Even the transport station was eerily vacant except for Freedom Force guards and the occasional person running late to work. It appeared all the citizens stayed home today if they didn't need to report in.

When they arrived at the Administration tower in their brown Reclamation uniforms, a guard at the building entrance leered at them. Lexi's heart rose into her throat, her hand squeezing Reeves's as if it were a flotation device on a sinking ship. She gave a somber nod to the guard as they passed. "Morning."

Rather than respond, the guard looked away, their brown uniforms apparently beneath him. She couldn't have asked for a better reaction.

Reeves tugged her toward the elevator that would take them to the greenhouse. "I don't know why, but this place is giving me the creeps."

She couldn't have said it better. The hairs on the back of her neck stood at attention as they ascended after selecting the top floor as their destination. Afraid the Imperium could hear them inside the elevator, she dropped her voice into whispered tones. "If Janie isn't there, I'm going to go, anyway. They said they'd give me access to the Favela. What's the worst that can happen? The door just won't open."

Looking sideways at her in an exasperated way, Reeves barely moved his lips when he responded. "The worst that could happen is the Freedom Force finds you trying to get in where you don't belong and executes us both."

He *would* have to spell it out like that. She sucked in a deep breath, and he squeezed her hand.

"I can't let it go." Her throat ached with trying to keep her voice quiet. How tempting to speak at a normal volume, as if she didn't care who heard what. "Aponi didn't deserve what they did to her. All she wanted was a family to love. She bought into the Imperium's fake dream. Thought she could marry the perfect man, hand selected for her, make lots of babies, and retire in luxury."

The elevator door opened to the sunlit greenhouse level. The sun shone so brightly, she had to squint until her eyes adjusted.

Reeves guided her through the door into the glass enclosure. A wave of heat sucked her in, and the air, heavy with moisture, caused each breath to clog her lungs.

They stalked the aisles, one at a time, searching for Janie. Each worker they passed either eyed them in suspicion or avoided eye contact as if they were dangerous. Until Reeves jerked her to a stop. "We'd have to be blind not to see everyone's on edge today. I'm worried someone will get too nervous at seeing Reclamation uniforms in the Administration building and call the guards to check us out."

"But this is the only greenhouse in the Imperium everyone can visit." She wouldn't let him derail their plans. "I've seen every color uniform in here over the years. It's normal to see

164

a Reclamation uniform touring."

A worker passed them, tapping commands into his tablet as he went.

Reeves waited until the guy had moved several paces away. "Not today, though. Everyone's afraid. Those who believe the bunk Tempest preached are terrified. Anyone who looks out of place might be a traitor." He nodded past her down the aisle, then back the other way. "Those who didn't buy in are worried they'll be next if the Imperium has even the slightest suspicion they're affiliated with the rebels. They'll do anything to prove they're all in with the Imperium—they'd turn their grandmama in for looking cross-eyed at a guard."

Reeves couldn't be far from the truth. No one smiled. Every look or lack thereof spoke volumes about the paranoia level. "Then let's stop looking for Janie and head down to the Favela ourselves. Now."

They moved toward the maintenance exit Janie had taken them through multiple times. Once in front of the door, they stood with their backs against it, surveying the room to ensure no one watched. Both took their watches off and stowed them behind the potted banana tree.

"This is it." Her heart thrummed a wicked beat in her chest. "If they didn't get my palm print into the security system for access, we're going to be stuck behind these doors until someone rescues or arrests us. You sure you want to go?"

He surveyed the room a final time before he answered with action—he pushed through the door and pulled her along. They were in.

"I sure hope your friends are still alive and not in hiding." He raced beside her down the stairwell. "Or this is going to be more excitement packed into one day than either of us wants."

She held up a hand for him to stop. "Listen." Footsteps echoed above them. "What should we say to anyone we run into?"

"We should have come up with a story *before* we went through those doors. What would make the most sense? That we're lost?"

She rolled her eyes. "Lame." Her voice came out in a whisper while the steps drew closer to the landing they stood on. "How about looking for Janie?"

He pursed his lips, his eyes narrowing. "We don't want to out her if we get caught and they don't believe us."

The person descending could only be a few flights above them now. Between the pounding of her heart and her rapid breaths, she might vomit. Or pass out. Most likely both.

When the steps paused, she held her breath. A door creaked open above them. Then a beat later, the click of it shutting reached them. Not trusting their good fortune, she counted to five. No more footsteps. "I think they're gone." She started back down the stairway, doing her best to move with as little sound as possible, yet eager to reach the bottom.

Reeves grabbed her arm. "You sure you still want to do this? We don't have any good reason to be here."

Of course, he was right. "We can't get out now except through access doors. If Y didn't get my palm scan in, we're stuck. Might as well try it at the door we *want* to go out. Right?"

He tipped his chin forward, and they continued to the bottom, then through the maze of hallways to the door Janie had taken them through before.

The palm reader glowed like a beacon as if begging Lexi to try her access rights.

"Go big or go home." She held her palm up, then mashed it

on the panel. "Please work."

During the microsecond the scanner read her palm, her heart thundered. Her palm, slick with sweat, slid on the scanner a beat before it flashed green and the latch clicked in release.

"Yes." The word came out like the hiss of a rattlesnake. *Time to strike.* Without a backward glance, she pushed open the door and eased out into the Favela. "Come on."

Reeves trailed her with an occasional touch to her shoulder or elbow. Her heart warmed in his presence—he had her back as they slunk along the buildings, down alleyways, and through rubble.

She paused in a recessed doorway and mashed in close to him. "Where are all the homeless? The Freedom Force must have carted more people off the streets than they showed on the vis."

He shrugged. "Or everyone's holed up out of sight. We may not find Ms. Becky. Especially if she doesn't want to be found."

"She's a friend—Nana's best friend if what she said last time is true." Lexi's stomach churned. "No. We can trust her. If she's out here, we'll find her."

A vehicle rumbled toward them. They pressed their backs tight against the building to disappear into its shadow. A Freedom Force van rounded a corner and crawled past them on the other side of the road. Two guards trailed the van, scanning the street and buildings as they moved. A drone hovered above them, circling.

Reeves moved closer to the corner wall where the shadow loomed larger. He took her hand, and doing her best not to make any sudden movements, she eased in next to him. He hugged her tight against him as her head lay on his chest.

She held her breath, clasped his hand, and listened to his

heart's rapid thrum. With his fingers intertwined with hers, the rhythm of her heart oddly matched his. *Focus, Lexi. Focus.*

"Hey." One guard hollered from the street.

She jumped, ready to dash, but Reeves's powerful arms held her tight. His breath tickled her ear. "Wait."

The guards took off running down a side street, followed by the van. She stood in his embrace, letting his scent of spiced herbs soothe her.

Then her breath came out in a whoosh, and she slid down the building until she rested on her haunches. "That was close."

He patted her shoulder. "Come on. We can't stop now. We need to keep moving."

This time, he led the way. A possessive hand clamped onto hers as if he feared losing her. They scurried up another alley with the guards' shouts fading.

The creak of a door opening came from behind them. Before she could turn, a beefy hand clamped on her shoulder and dragged her backward while another hand fastened over her mouth to silence the screech she let fly.

Reeves spun to face her, eyes wide and fists up and ready to strike. Then his fighting stance collapsed, and his arms dropped to his side. "It's you."

Lexi tipped her head back to see Fletcher's watermelon-sized one above hers. She sagged against his hold.

He released her and motioned them inside. "Come on. Ms. Becky is waiting."

This time, they moved through an old department store. Enormous holes in an exterior wall let in the sunshine, so they made their way without tripping over abandoned mannequins picked clean of their clothes long ago.

Near the back, behind what had once been a sales counter,

Fletcher walked them through a door into a ramshackle office. Ms. Becky sat at a rusted-over metal desk, her face distorted by the strange shadows the oil lamp threw off.

Janie popped out of an unlit corner. "You made it."

Lexi couldn't help but smile back. They *had* made it. This time on their own. They were getting good at this being-a-rebel thing. "I'm ready to help. Just tell me what to do, and I'm in."

Janie fist-pumped. "That's what I'm talking about."

Fletcher harrumphed.

Ms. Becky beamed. "I'd hoped you'd follow in your nana's footsteps. You look so much like her. I can almost imagine she's still with us when I see you."

That brought an ache to Lexi's chest. "I wish I could have saved her."

"You can do the next best thing." Ms. Becky waved her over to sit in an old metal chair probably too rusty to hold a sparrow, much less a person. "I have a mission for you, but it'll be dangerous. I can't guarantee your safety."

The time had come. Did she trust Ms. Becky enough to follow her? Lexi eyed the chair and decided.

She sat.

The chair creaked but held. Reeves stepped up behind her and placed his hands on her shoulders. Without thinking, she reached a hand up to cover his. It was as if power flowed from his hand to hers, strengthening her. Funny how this felt normal. She squared her shoulders. "Just tell me what to do."

"The Imperium has scheduled a trip to Solitude for another batch of retirees. Normally, Janie is good at gathering intel, but our sources tell us her access in and out of the Favela was cut yesterday as part of the sweep." Ms. Becky rubbed Janie's back. "I can't allow her back inside the Imperium. It's too much of a risk now. But your father should know the plans from his work in Administration. We need you to find out when it's leaving."

Lexi's stomach fell. They were going to bomb the transportation hub again. How did that make them any better than the Imperium? "No. I won't help you kill innocent people."

Ms. Becky winced. "I'm so sorry about your mom. It was so unfair for her to die that way. But I promise you, what happened had nothing to do with me. With us." Her glare pinned Janie to the spot as if this was the continuation of a previous conversation. "See the pain violence causes? Do you want that?"

Janie fixed her focus on the floor and kicked at debris.

But Lexi's jangled nerves remained unsettled until the squeeze of Reeves's hand calmed her. "Then why do you need to know when they're leaving? The Imperium keeps the schedule secret to protect the retirees. My grandparents didn't deserve to die, either."

Ms. Becky returned her full attention to Lexi, then leaned back in her chair, and laced her bony fingers on her lap. "The Imperium is lying to you. Lying to all its citizens. Your father knows this as much as I do. This falsehood is the foundation of why we must rebel—it's the purpose of Y."

Lexi's heart froze. Now they were getting somewhere. "I'm listening."

"There is no retirement. Solitude doesn't exist."

The world stopped spinning. Lexi's brain couldn't digest this. "But... the transports take the retirees to Solitude. If it doesn't exist, where are they all going?"

Janie stormed out of the room, shoving Fletcher away when

he tried to block her.

Ms. Becky shook her head. "Let her go."

Lexi's no-longer-frozen heart might explode out of her chest from hammering against her rib cage. She closed her eyes and squeezed Reeves's hand with all her remaining strength. Warring thoughts vied for dominance. She wanted to know the truth. Didn't she? But the possibilities terrified her. Her voice dipped, barely audible. "The retirees. Where are they going?"

Ms. Becky's tone hardened. "They kill them. *Every. One.*"

Chapter 19

Someone had sucked the air out of the room. Lexi couldn't breathe. She must have heard wrong. No way would anyone systemically wipe out a generation for the simple fact that they'd reached retirement age and were no longer useful.

She needed to walk, to escape. But when she tried to stand, her knees buckled, and she sank to the floor.

Reeves rushed around the chair and stooped down beside her. His voice sounded distorted, like he was at the far end of a long tunnel. "Breathe, Lexi. Look at me. Deep breaths."

Her world went gray around the edges. She *couldn't* breathe. There was no air. Hands were on her face, so warm, almost hot. Fingers moved her head—fuzzy images floated in front of her.

"Lexi. Focus." Reeves's face drifted into view. "Let's slow those breaths down now. Okay. Breathe in. One. Two. Three." The space around her solidified.

That wasn't so bad. I can do that.

He spoke again. "Perfect. Good job. Now let's slow down the exhale next time."

His lips came into focus. *My oh my, he has amazing lips.*

"Breathe in. One. Two. Three. And out. One. Two. Three."

Ms. Becky had gotten up from her chair and stood behind him. "Sorry. I should have been more tactful."

Ignoring Ms. Becky, Reeves patted Lexi's hands. "You're doing great, Lexi. Had me worried there for a minute." He huffed out a laugh. "I didn't know you could turn that white. Did you know you had a freckle right here?" He touched the tip of her nose.

What an idiot she'd been. Did she think it would be all sunshine and rainbows if she joined Y?

She shook her head. "Help me up."

Reeves stood, then lifted her with both of his hands.

Her brain spun, but with her next blink and another deep breath—and with Reeves's arms around her waist—the room settled back into place. Since her legs continued to quake, she opted to take the rickety chair once again. It moaned its dissatisfaction as she sank onto it.

She held a shaky hand toward Ms. Becky. "Why would the Imperium kill the retirees? It doesn't make any sense."

Ms. Becky sat on the edge of her desk. "Back when our city existed as part of a greater nation, resources overflowed. Never equally, mind you. The rich and the poor always existed, though there was class division. But the wealthy and the government redistributed some of the abundance so the poor didn't starve."

Like the times her mother had taken protein bars to the Favela to give to those who lived on the edge of survival. Imperium citizens were all assigned jobs at either seventeen or nineteen if their roles were higher level. The Imperium showed the door to those who didn't fit into its perfect society. Abandoned them to figure out survival on their own. "What does that have to do with the elderly?"

"Everything hummed along fine in our city until a wave of retirements happened. People who held enough wealth stopped working and lived off the resources they'd saved. Many possessed enough to live comfortably until their deaths and still leave money for the next generation to inherit."

The Administration buildings had never been luxurious, but Lexi lived like a queen when she compared it with the Favela. Others must see her as one of the current wealthy. "People retire. Once you get to a certain age, we still do." But in the Imperium retirement really meant… *death*. "When did they decide to kill off everyone who wanted to retire?"

"People started retiring at younger and younger ages. Why work, they thought, if we can get by on less?" Ms. Becky moved back to her chair, rested her elbows on the desk, and put her chin on her hands. "Soon there were too many retired and not enough to work the factories, the stores, or even the massive farms feeding the people. Many of those who retired didn't have the resources to take care of themselves as they aged. Health care had improved to where we lived longer lives—much longer."

"But that's a good thing." Lexi's legs itched. She needed to move. "Longer lives give us time to be there for our grandchildren. Why not just let everyone be? I'd have slept on the couch the rest of my life to keep Nana and Gramps in my life."

"You were lucky to spend time with your grandparents, but by this time, people were having fewer children. People adopted pets rather than take on the responsibility of bringing up the next generation."

No longer able to sit still, Lexi stood, ignoring Reeves's hand as he reached for her. His concern made her want to go back to their apartment and stay there—shut the world, the Imperium, out of their lives forever. Emotions swam through her. Jittery and unsettled, she waved both arms indicating everything and nothing in particular. "Some idiot decided to start knocking people off? What did that solve?"

A bitter laugh huffed out, and Ms. Becky sat back in her chair. "Nothing's as easy as that. As time went on, fewer and fewer young people were doing the work. Certainly not enough to care for the elderly and run the world at the same time. People lived longer and longer, but their lives weren't necessarily healthier. They needed more care, more help just to get out of bed in the morning, much less eat and bathe."

"Stand still." Fletcher growled. "You're making me nervous."

Oops. She'd been pacing around Reeves. She sat again. "Sorry."

"The long and the short of it is that we could no longer do both. Caring for the elderly and keeping the supply chains moving became too difficult. When those chains broke under the pressure, the wars took out most of the elderly, along with a good portion of the young. Afterward, those in power decided they could never allow the situation to occur again. They instituted 'retirement' in a different location where the elderly would have to care for themselves. Then it became easier to eliminate them rather than ship them off."

And the assignment Ms. Becky wanted her to take on...? "What is Y doing about it? Why do you want to know when the next retirees are leaving?"

"We do our best to save as many as we can. Mostly through abduction of the unsuspecting. We tell them the truth, and if they agree to it, they join us in the Favela. We give them a chance to live out the rest of the lives they've been given, but

175

it's not an easy life."

If only Mom could have rescued Nana and Gramps. Something didn't make sense though. "If Mom knew the truth, why was she on her way to the transport with Nana and Gramps? Shouldn't she have brought them here?" Ms. Becky closed her eyes, her shoulders slumping. Bowing her head, she rubbed her temples and breathed in and out in silence. When she raised her head, her eyes glistened. "She should have. All I've been able to figure out is that she meant to make it look like they were being compliant but planned to use the opportunity to rescue others from the transport area before bringing everyone here. But the bomb ended her efforts."

The explosion came rushing back, ticking Lexi's heart rate back up. "You said your people didn't set it off. Who did? Who set off the bomb?"

Fletcher, normally content to let Ms. Becky lead the conversation, stepped in. "All we know is it's a faction of Y. Those who aren't satisfied with rescue and protection. Their influence is potent, especially with the young ones like Janie. They're tired of waiting for the Imperium to change its ways and want to force it. It was their work that day."

"You see?" Ms. Becky slapped the table, half rising in her seat on the steam of passion. "The war will start again if we allow our current paths to continue. I don't want a war. Peace is our only way forward. But that takes time. Help me save as many as I can for now."

Could Lexi hope to convince her father? He hadn't listened to her mother. Why would he listen to her? This would take a plan. "I need to think about it." She tucked her hand through Reeves's arm. "Let's go home."

He stepped closer to Ms. Becky. "I've got one last question.

What does Y stand for? I've been trying to think of every *Y* word I can that would mean rebellion or some such, but I can't figure it out."

Fletcher harrumphed. "Told you we needed to change it."

After a glare at her protector, Ms. Becky smiled at Reeves. "You may not realize it, but at one time, there were many beliefs in unseen beings. One group followed a man who claimed to be God. His name in an ancient language called Hebrew was Yeshua."

Reeves's eyes narrowed. "Why would you name your rebellion after a crazy man who thought himself to be a god?"

Ms. Becky shrugged. "A group of his followers lived in the ancient Roman cities. The Romans would discard children they didn't want by 'exposing' them. They'd drop them off at the edge of the woods, unwanted. Their form of birth control, I suppose." She shook her head. "Those who followed Yeshua's teachings would rescue the infants and raise them as their own. Since we also rescue the discarded and some of us secretly follow the teachings of Yeshua, we've taken up his symbol."

Lexi slid her hand down Reeve's arm to grasp his fingers. Nana's explanation of the necklace came back. This group must be some sort of cult, trying to bring religion back to life against the Imperium rules. Truly insane. And yet, she couldn't fault them for their goals of protecting the retirees.

Her day had begun only hours ago. Exhaustion already weighed on her as if she'd lived two full days without rest. With a squeeze of Reeves's hand, she got his attention. "Ready to go?"

He nodded, and they turned to the door.

"Please," Ms. Becky said from behind them. "Don't take too long to think about our request. Those people haven't a chance

177

if we don't help them. No one deserves to be put down just because they've reached a certain age."

Though she didn't turn back, Lexi paused. "We'll think about it."

They dodged a few Freedom Force patrols on their way back to the Administration tower, but none of the locals. Had the Imperium captured all the people in the Favela who weren't rebels? Or had the homeless become experts in hiding? One could hope for the latter.

Her palm print granted them access back into the building, and they managed a quick return to the greenhouse to retrieve their watches.

On their way home, she clung to his arm as if he were a life ring tossed into the ocean of emotions pulling her under. He'd been as silent as she had, but he held her close. Perhaps he needed as much reassurance from her as she from him.

Fresh waves of sorrow rolled through her mind at the loss of Mom, Nana, and Gramps. Knowing what the Imperium did to retirees added another level of grief.

She'd never known her father's parents. They'd retired before Lexi was born. A bitter laugh escaped, drawing Reeves's attention as they neared their apartment.

"What?" He squeezed her closer. "Share with the rest of the class, because I sure could use something funny right now."

Once they were alone and out of the hallway, they could talk freely. She pulled a glass out of the cabinet. "There's nothing amusing about any of this, but I just realized my father's parents aren't off living in Solitude someplace. They're dead, and he knows it. He knew Nana and Gramps were next and never lifted a finger to save them."

He leaned against the kitchen counter with his arms crossed

as if in deep contemplation. "How do you know? Maybe he helped with the plan to get them out, along with your mom. Even though the rebels ruined your mom's plan, whatever it was, doesn't mean your dad hadn't helped somehow."

She filled the glass with water and took a sip while she let the thought roll around in her brain, testing it to see if it fit. Doubtful. But… Whoa. Why hadn't she thought of *that* before? "Mom's diary. We didn't finish it. Let's skip forward and see what she wrote."

She reclaimed her backpack and dug through it for the diary. Together, they sat on the couch as she paged to the last entry.

> *Lexi,*
>
> *I hope it's you who opens this diary. Every entry, every thought I've jotted down so you would know how much I love you. I can't let your nana and gramps go, though my heart aches at the risk of losing you as well.*
>
> *If we're caught and someone else reads this, know that my daughter knew nothing. She's innocent. But if it is you, my beautiful, smart, and only child, know I'm doing this for all of us, not just for them. Someday, you'll know the truth, and I don't want you to wonder why I stood by and allowed them to die. Instead, you must know I acted to save them. Just like you would have.*
>
> *I love you forever.*
> *Mom*

Nothing about her father's involvement. Did the fact mean something? Or had she left his name out to protect him if the diary fell into other hands?

Frustration frazzled Lexi's nerves. "We're only going to

know if he was involved is if we ask him."

"Do you think he'd be honest if we did?"

Fair point. Her father hadn't been the most forthcoming person in her life. It didn't help that he acted the oil to her water—no easy way to put them together.

And yet... Raising her chin, she set her heart on the task. "I have to try."

Chapter 20

Lexi's legs ached as if she'd run a marathon. She and Reeves had spent more time walking from building to transport station—and then through more buildings— in one day than she would have in an entire week. When he reached for her hand, she realized her arms burned as well. Stress must be throwing a party in her body.

They'd taken seats in the tram, and their car remained empty except for them. Still, she couldn't help but whisper, fearful the Imperium heard everything, everywhere. "Am I bonkers right now? Is talking to my father the right move?"

Reeves leaned in close. With the way his lips moved close to her ear, any casual observer would've thought they shared lovers' secrets. "You know your father better than I do. Feel him out. See what he's thinking. Until you're confident, though, keep your plans discreet."

Even after her father knew, he'd wanted her to be a part of the Administration. Her shoulders slumped, and she leaned into Reeves. So much of what she'd learned since her graduation was hard to process.

Though Reeves had been in her life only three short days, it seemed as if he'd been beside her forever. His square jaw gave him an air of power, almost invincible. He'd been her rock, taking Mom's place as a lifeline to sanity.

His brilliant smile lit their car and broke the tension. "What?"

He must have seen her confusion, so he snuggled closer to whisper once more. "You're looking at me as if you're surprised I'm sitting here. What's going through that brain of yours?"

The tickle of his breath against her ear and neck sent a shiver down her spine. She nudged his ear down closer to her lips to return the favor. "I'm grateful to have you with me. Thank you for understanding."

Her breathy words had to have the same effect on him as goose bumps rose on his arm where it rested against her own.

Nana had told her stories about how people used to spend time together, getting to know each other before they decided whom they wanted to marry. They called it dating, back before the Imperium. Would it have been like this to date Reeves? The stolen glances, the heightened sense of closeness, the heart flutters when he was near. Only without the stress of knowing the Imperium was out to murder everyone she loved.

Way to kill the buzz, Lexi. She patted his hand as the tram slowed at the Administration building.

They disembarked and headed toward the elevators to the residential sector. Freedom Force guards swarmed the transport area as if they expected more trouble. Reeves shrugged after Lexi gave him the what's-up look.

Then they saw it. Painters were busy covering graffiti. A painter had already hidden half of a Y bird symbol behind a fresh coat of paint, but the rest was plain to see. Lexi squeezed Reeves's hand as if she could pull more strength through his arm.

She wanted to scream out her frustration—to grab the sprayer from the painter's hands and stop the work to hide the symbol. If she had a can of spray paint and even an ounce of the talent for art Janie did, she'd march over to the Imperium's lackey and redo the work he'd destroyed.

A guard stepped up to them, huge rifle in hand. "State your business in the Administration building."

Fear skittered down her spine. Had he noticed her staring at the symbol? Did he suspect they didn't approve of the Imperium's cover-up?

Reeves's voice filled the void her racing brain couldn't. "My wife's father is in Administration. She recently graduated with an assignment in Reclamation." He plastered on a genuine-looking smile. "We're still on our honeymoon. Going to check in with the family. You know." He even added a wink as if to drive his point home.

"Administration is in lockdown." The guard pushed them both backward a step. "Unless you have official business, you need to head to your tower. *Now*."

Lexi's breath faltered as her heart thrummed in her chest. More had to be going on than this minor act of vandalism.

A scream echoed through the transport station. A petite woman in a green gardener's uniform struggled to wrench away from a guard who held her. Her hat flapped with her efforts. Another guard pulled his Taser and shot her in the chest the moment she'd freed herself. She fell to the cement floor, shuddering under the electric assault.

Reeves gripped Lexi's elbow. "We understand, officer. We're heading back to Reclamation now."

Lexi stumbled, but Reeves's powerful arms dragged and carried her to the waiting tram, even while she focused on the woman on the floor. After the compact figure stopped shuddering, the guards scooped up her limp form and hauled her across the platform, past the tram's open door.

A gasp escaped Lexi's lips when she confirmed what she'd been thinking but refused to admit—the person in tow was Janie. Reeves pressed her hand in a way that reminded Lexi not to draw attention. She knew better, but the desire to jump out of the tram to defend her friend overwhelmed her.

Reeves's hot breath pulsed into her ear with his whisper. "There's nothing we can do for her now. You need to let it go."

Fighting the urge to ignore him, she closed her eyes as a tear escaped. She used her free hand to swipe it away. *There must be something I can do. Anything.*

The tram's doors slid shut, and they were off toward the Reclamation building. She held it together, clinging to Reeves's arm, letting him be her life ring again until they made it behind the closed doors of their apartment.

Then she fell apart.

At first, she broke down in tears, sobbing at the fast-accumulating losses. Reeves embraced her, his closeness comforting her. "It's going to be okay. We'll figure something out."

His words struck her as all sorts of wrong. Heat sizzled through her, and she pushed him away, swiping her sleeve across her face. "No. It's not *okay*. None of this is *okay*."

He stepped back and held up both hands to ward off the blow of her words. "I didn't say it *was* okay. I said it'll *be* okay."

"They kill people as if it's a sport. They'll do the same to Janie." She stormed through the kitchen, picked up a glass from the sink, and smashed it onto the floor. The scattered fragments brought a sense of accomplishment, pitiful as it was.

Then the failed mission—to speak to her father—overwhelmed her. She sank to her knees, allowing a sliver of glass to penetrate her jumpsuit. She indulged in the pain instead of fleeing from it. "They'll kill all those retirees too if we can't figure out when they're leaving. We have to get the date and their names so Y can save them."

Reeves walked to the vacuum panel and set the bot to clean the kitchen. It scurried out of its hideaway and swept up the debris she'd created. He followed the bot's path and reached out to her.

She released a growl, then accepted his help. When he pulled her into an embrace, she let his arms be her strength.

He rubbed her shoulders. "We'll figure it out."

She eased back to view his face. "I'm sorry I dragged you into this. Knowing my luck, I'll be the next one on the vis. If you stick with me, you'll be there too."

He shook his head. "You've opened my eyes in more ways than one." He slid his hands down her arms, then entwined their fingers. "Now that I know what's going on, I couldn't turn away, even if you did."

So, he was in. All the way. Her knees almost buckled under a strange combination of appreciation—and terror. Aponi had been right. Reeves could fill in her holes. Make her more solid than she already was.

She might very well be his undoing.

But there wasn't time to worry about that now. The next set of retirees might have only hours left. They had to get her father to help. "Maybe my father will come to us since we aren't going to get into Administration anytime soon."

She tapped a message on her watch, reading it aloud to Reeves. "How's this sound? 'Tried to visit today. Come see us.'"

"That's basic enough. Nothing there to concern the Imperium. You think he'll come?"

With a shrug, she tugged her sleeve over her watch. "He has to. If not, I can't figure any other way to get to him."

Both their watches buzzed and flashed. Another message from the Imperium.

Required viewing for all Imperium citizens in fifteen minutes. Please find your closest vis unit.

A weight dropped into her stomach from the stone they'd be forced to swallow. Would there be more arrests of innocent Favela dwellers? She scowled at the vis screen as if it had a life of its own and stalked her for enjoyment. "I can't watch."

Reeves moved to stand between her and the unit. "Don't then. Go into the bedroom. I'll tell you if it's anything you need to know about."

What if they planned to televise more executions? The stone in her gut morphed into lava, and her insides heaved. She dashed toward the bathroom in time to disgorge what little her stomach held. Her brain mustn't have gotten the message from her digestive system—there wasn't anything in there. Round after round of dry heaves followed.

When her brain flew the white flag and gave up, she rinsed her mouth and splashed cool water over her face. She almost expected steam to come off her flushed face. Instead, the mirror's mottled reflection seemed to have lost its soul.

The Imperium's announcement introduction music came from the living room. The four mottos would be flowing across the screen to remind them of the prison walls they lived within.

Unity above all else.

Sure. They were united, all right. Right down to their shackles.

Hard work lifts us all.

Their backs would break under the Imperium's demands.

A young Imperium is a thriving Imperium.

And not a drop of the wisdom age could bring them would survive.

One marriage—many children.

Whether you wanted it or not.

She had left the bathroom door open in her haste. Now the vis screen's light reflected off Reeves's face. Colors danced across his eyes as he stared at the images.

Oddly, his expression drew her to him as if she could watch the vis through his eyes and see his thoughts. Feel what he felt.

Without a glance at the vis, she walked over and slid her hand into his. Alarms sounded in her brain with his sharp intake of breath and viselike grip. His face fell, eyes creasing. It was as if he couldn't look away, though he wanted to.

Tempest Malachy's voice invaded their home. "The Imperium's Freedom Force has triumphed once again. A hardened rebel bent on the destruction of our great city walked into the trap our guards set for her. We can all rejoice because they have plucked one more thorn from our collective side."

Lexi didn't need to see the vis. Reeves's eyes indicated the screen showed some poor schlep being paraded out as a trophy. Her world turned upside down when he whispered. "Janie."

Her first response was to lean against his chest and wrap her arms around him, desperate for comfort in what would come next.

Tempest's voice almost crooned. "Justice remains swift in the Imperium. We will not tolerate rebels determined to break the will of the people."

His muscled arms shook against her. He'd seen enough. Her

hands framed his face and forced his gaze on hers.

His eyes were unfocused, not seeming to recognize her or perhaps mentally stuck in the image he'd witnessed. "Look at me."

He gazed at her, searching as if he'd find the answer to a puzzle. "We're going to do something about this. No more waiting for someone else to fix it." As he spoke, her fingers ached with the pressure she was certain he wasn't aware he was using on her. "Promise me."

Not taking her eyes off his, she returned the pressure. "I promise."

She'd fallen into the infinite depths of his blue eyes when the firing squad's eruption came out of the vis.

Chapter 21

Lexi woke, stiff and sore from a restless night. When she tried to sit up, an arm held her in place, and alarm shot through her—until she remembered she'd fallen asleep beside Reeves. He snuffled in his sleep and rolled to his other side. Doing her best not to wake him, she slid from under the comforter and eased off the bed.

She'd never slept with anyone before, yet already, she missed the comfortable warmth his body provided. She stared back at her husband—*husband*, still a foreign concept.

One leg of his uniform had worked its way up to his knee, and his hair looked as though he'd slept through a tornado. Her jumpsuit was a wrinkled mess. Who knew how long it would take to feel comfortable sleeping as a husband and wife should, in night attire or not? Last night, they'd only known they didn't want to be apart, so they lay together, fully clothed, talking until their throats had grown too tired to speak another word. She'd never felt so close to another soul.

She padded into the bathroom to shower and prepare for another crazy day. As insane as the last week had been, no way would today be normal. Now that she knew the truth, life would never be normal again.

The shower still dripped from its recent use when the

doorbell called to her. She rushed to pull on a fresh uniform and drag a brush through her soggy locks. A tap on the bathroom door interrupted.

"Your father's here." Reeves's groggy voice came across as if he'd jumped out of bed half asleep to get the door.

Her father had come!

"I'll be out in a minute." Tension over the conversation to come chased away her relief. She stared herself down in the mirror. *Don't get upset. No matter what. You need his help.*

Her father, dressed in his usual suit, stood up from the couch when she exited the bathroom. Tired eyes peered above a clenched jaw. "We need to talk, young lady."

Great. Something already had him wound up. This was *not* how the conversation needed to start. "Good morning to you too."

When he closed his eyes and sucked in a deep breath, she recognized his move to calm himself. "I don't think you understand the position you're putting me in—putting our family in."

"Our *family*?" What relatives did they have besides the two of them? She tried to pin him to the wall with a glare.

His words came out through gritted teeth. "Your husband? My wife?"

Reeves, wide awake now, leaned against the kitchen counter, arms crossed. This wasn't going well. *Slow down, Lexi. You need him.* Her feet, still bare from the shower, slapped soggy patterns on the bamboo floor. "I'm sorry. I wasn't thinking."

Good. Her apology brought the needed effect. Dad let out his breath with a nod. "I'm sorry too. I shouldn't have come at you like that." He shoved his hands into his pockets. "I'm worried about you. About us." He stepped closer. "You aren't safe. I saw you in the Favela."

Her head snapped up. The subject she'd been pondering how to broach, the retirees, fled. "What do you mean? How?"

"I'm on the security task force. The image was grainy, so I doubt anyone who didn't know you well would have recognized you. I saw you from my view screen when I was manning a drone."

Right. The drone patrolling with the guards. What were the odds her father had been running it? It didn't matter. She stiffened her back. "We were there for a reason. That's why we needed to talk to you."

"No. What you *need* is to stay out of the Favela. *That's* what we need to talk about." His jaw clenched again.

Need. Need. Need. His emphasis on the word stuck on repeat. *She* needed him to focus on the problem. "I know about the retirees. I know what the Imperium does to them."

His eyes went wide, and his lips pursed as if to keep him from saying the first thing that came to mind.

"Sir?" Reeves broke the silence. "Sir, *we need* your help to save the next group of retirees. Lexi and I can protect them—if you'll assist us."

Her father's eyes narrowed on him as if he'd found a fresh target. "*You need* to keep my daughter away from the rebels, not encourage her."

Heat flared in her chest. "Reeves and I are a team. Something you wouldn't understand, seeing how you left Mom out on her own with Nana and Gramps. If you'd been there for her, she might still be alive."

He flinched, but then his face reddened. "Your mother wouldn't listen to me any more than you do. I tried to tell her to stay away from those crazy Y rebels. It should be obvious

191

to you which one of us was right. I'm standing in front of you. Where is she?"

A bitter laugh exploded out of her mouth. "My point exactly. You care about one person—yourself."

She bit the inside of her mouth as the color of his face deepened and a purple vein on his forehead bulged. This wasn't going the way she needed it to. There was that word again—*need*.

Reeves moved away from the counter, closer to her father. "Look. Let's not fight. We all want to be safe, and we all want to do what's best. Right?"

His calm demeanor soothed her. Perhaps she should have let him take the lead in this. Her relationship with her father had always been complicated. Like two bulls fighting for dominance. "Reeves is right. We need—must—work together."

For a beat, they waited for her father's response. He took a deep breath. "I don't want to argue, but if you think I'm going to hand over a list of names and dates, you've got another think coming." He jammed a finger at her. "That sort of thing got your mother killed. I won't have a target painted on our foreheads because you want to save the world."

Mom's diary... Hadn't Mom said... Lexi stepped closer, touching her father's hand. Mom said Dad wanted reform by changing the Imperium from the inside out. Maybe a different approach would have the right effect. "What if I agree to retake the test? To annul my marriage and return to the engineering program, will you help me out with this one last request?"

Reeves took in a sharp breath. She couldn't make eye contact. The pain she glimpsed in his cut too deep. She'd explain her reasoning later, but for now, she must focus on getting her father to help.

With his nod, his jaw relaxed. "What do you need?"

Need. The word rankled her again.

Yet she didn't dare waste another second. "We *need* a list of names for the next set of retirees and the date they'll board the trams to Solitude."

Head cocked to one side, he apparently considered her request. "If I agree to this, I'll expect you to test again—immediately. It may already be too late since your honeymoon is almost over, but I've got a few favors I can still call in." He cleared his throat. "No offense, son. You'd have been a good husband, but my daughter belongs in Administration."

Reeves didn't answer. Instead, he stalked into the bedroom. The door slammed shut.

Lexi's chest ached. Hearts didn't really break, did they? She didn't want to hurt Reeves. He'd understand once she explained. He had to.

She held her chin high. "When can you get me the list?"

"Soon." Her father moved toward the door, a smirk in place. "But you must stay out of the Favela. They're going to clear it all out, Lexi. They'll label anyone there as an enemy of the people. If your rebels want the list, make *them* come to *you*."

The way he talked, you'd think she had Y on a leash. She'd have laughed out loud if the truth wasn't so frightening. "I'll see if I can make that happen."

His hand was on the doorknob. "Look for an encrypted message from me. I'll use your date of birth, in reverse, as the password. It'll have the information you need. Pass the data on, then say goodbye to your friends. You and I will take this on together, as we should have all along. *My* way."

Clamping her lips together, she bit her tongue on the words that came to mind. His condescending attitude stirred rather

193

unkind thoughts.

At her nod, he left.

Alone in her living room, she took slow breaths. Her heart hammered, but she didn't blame it for going crazy. What had just happened? She'd pulled her father in to help with the rebellion he didn't agree with. She'd agreed to annul her marriage and go back to the job she dreaded. But worst of all, she'd hurt the one person still alive she cared about.

She closed her eyes, the deep, calming breaths failing to do their job. Reeves didn't deserve the pain her family dished out.

Before she could go to him, the bedroom door opened, and he came back into the room, hands in his pockets, expression unreadable. "He's gone?"

She nodded, her chest aching at the distance between them. The gap seemed insurmountable. "He said he'd help."

His lips pursed while his eyes focused on the floor. "That's good. What you wanted."

Unable to take the separation any longer, she hurried over and slid her arms down his as she'd done before. When she got to the ends of them, instead of allowing her to grasp his hands, he jerked away and kept his hands in his pockets.

The stab to her heart was sharp, like a knife wound. He didn't resist when she wrapped her arms around his waist and laid her head on his chest. "I'm sorry. I have no intention of following through with it. But I had to get him to help us. It was the only way."

He huffed out a laugh, slid his hands out of his pockets, and wrapped his arms around her. "Maybe you should do what he says. Reclamation isn't going to give you anywhere near what life in Administration could. Who knows? They might reassign you after you finish school to marry some high-ranking council member. Better than picking through trash for the rest of your life with me."

The knife in her heart twisted. She lifted her head. "You think I want that? You're the best thing to happen to me in years. I can't do this without you."

A fierce glare hit her hard when his eyes met hers. "Of course you can. When we were reading your mom's diary, it could have been your own. You're just like her. Brave. Courageous. Ready to take on the Imperium and save the lives of people you don't even know."

He pressed her tighter into himself, muffling the sob she let escape. The cocoon of his arms spread warmth through her body, and she indulged in the sensation as she reined in her emotions.

His eyes came into focus after she swiped away the tears. He brushed his lips against hers—featherlight.

Her lips buzzed, wanting more. "Don't you dare leave me. You promised you'd support me. Remember?"

His sad smile didn't help soothe her hurt. "That I did. And I will." He cleared his throat. "You have to make me a promise as well."

Right now, she'd do anything to make his smile genuine again. "Name it."

"Promise me you'll do what you need to do to stay safe. Stay alive. No matter what."

She gave his arm a gentle slap. "You make it sound as if I have some sort of death wish or something. I guarantee you—I want to see tomorrow just as much as the next gal."

He tucked a strand of her hair behind her ear. "I'm not sure why, but I get the feeling you'll need to make a choice someday soon. A choice to live or die. Promise me you'll choose to live."

That didn't seem like a difficult decision. Who would choose to die when living was an option? Lexi Verity was no martyr. "Of course. I promise."

"Thank you." His breath warmed her ear as he squeezed her close. "I'll hold you to that."

Chapter 22

L exi must have checked her messages a hundred times in the two hours after her father left. She jumped off the couch and headed toward the kitchen for her third drink of water. Though none of the previous attempts to clear the lump in her throat had been successful, it didn't hurt to try once more. She paced their kitchen. "He should have sent something by now."

Reeves remained on the couch, scrolling through the public archives. "You need to be patient. Who knows how long it'll take him to get the data?"

A knock rumbled on the front door. She jumped and choked on her sip of water, then croaked out a question the moment her coughs subsided. "He said he'd send it electronically—right?"

Having already moved to the door, Reeves nodded, then activated the view screen to see who stood outside. "It's Rumi. Looks like she's been crying." His eyes narrowed on Lexi. "Be nice."

She bristled. "I'm always nice." The words came out like a snake's hiss. Perhaps he had a point. She moved to join her husband at the door and welcomed her father's young bride. "Are you okay? What happened?"

Rumi's swollen, red eyes still held tears, and she fidgeted with a cloth in her hand. "Gunner told me what he planned to do. I tried to talk him out of it." She marched into Lexi's space. "How could you ask him to do something so dangerous?"

If this wannabe replacement for Mom thought she could storm into their home and demand attention, Lexi would set her back in her place. She opened her mouth to start a lesson in respect.

But Reeves placed a hand on hers and spoke first. "I know it's stressful to see your husband in danger, but he's trying to save lives."

Fresh tears blossomed from Rumi's eyes. "I know. He cares more about those strangers than he does me." Shoulders slumping, she wiped her eyes with the twisted cloth. "He told me to come here. Said you'd keep me safe if something went wrong."

Lexi clamped her mouth on the first words that came to mind. *Great. Now I'm a glorified babysitter.* "You're welcome to stay here, but we've got some errands to run."

Reeves raised his brows. "We do?"

Why couldn't he just play along? "Yes, we do. We need to find another way into the Favela. Remember? We can't go back through the Administration building. It's in lockdown."

"No!" Rumi's eyes went wide, her hands, damp cloth and all, clawed at Lexi. "You can't go to the Favela. They're clearing it out. You'll be arrested and executed."

"Not to worry. I'd never let my wife do something as silly as that." Reeves's tone soothed as if trying to calm a frightened rabbit. He grabbed Lexi's arm and strode toward their bedroom, ignoring her struggles. "Lexi and I need to chat. Please make yourself at home, Rumi. We'll be back in a flash."

Once the bedroom door had closed behind them, Reeves spun her to face him. His eyes ablaze, his words came out in a harsh whisper. "Have you lost your ever-loving mind? We don't know which side Rumi is on. For all we know, she's in the pocket of a prominent council member—or even all of them. Why not share your plans with the council directly? It would save time."

Her heart thundered. She wanted to scream, but a niggling thought prevented her—he was right. She sucked in a breath and clenched her hands. "Sorry. I don't get why my father dumped her in our lap. We *must* get the list to the rebels the moment we get it. How are we supposed to do that if we've got to keep an eye on Mrs. Scaredy-Pants?"

His lips twitched as if restraining something. He cleared his throat. "You're an intelligent woman. Smart enough to be an engineer, from what the Imperium says. You can figure something out."

She sucked in a calming breath, then another. Another. "There must be maintenance doors into the Favela from all the buildings. We need to find the one in Reclamation. I'll bet it's down near the reclamation pits. The smells match up well enough."

This time, he didn't hold back his grin. "That's my girl." He snugged her into a hug, and the scent of spice herbs surrounded her. "Now. Can we go back out there and comfort your father's wife? It's not her fault the Imperium gave her to him."

Her heart lighter, she returned his embrace with a squeeze, then wiggled free. Before she could take their first step toward the door, her watch buzzed a message. "It's my father. Maybe it's the list."

She wriggled her tablet out of her backpack and opened the message files. Adrenaline brought on an electric buzz, causing her fingers to fumble as they tapped on the screen. "It's encrypted. I think this is it."

It took two attempts to get her birth date entered to open the email. The capitalization of the subject line made it easy to read for not only Lexi but also Reeves as he peered over her shoulder.

Her blood ran cold at the message.

THEY'RE ON THEIR WAY—GET OUT NOW!

Reeves wasted no time. He rushed out of the bedroom, Lexi at his heels, then yanked his watch off, and tossed it on the couch. He loomed over Rumi. "Give me your watch."

"Wh–why?" She backed away, eyes wide as she clamped a hand over her watch.

Lexi stripped off her own device and left it beside Reeves's. She held her palms toward Rumi, dropping her voice to a lower octave as if calming a savage beast. "The Imperium can track us with the watches. We're going to leave them here, so the Freedom Force assumes we're staying put."

Rumi backed against the door, shaking her head. "But how will Gunner find us if we leave?"

Reeves approached Rumi from the side as Lexi continued her more direct path. The girl's eyes were as wide as two full moons, and her breaths too shallow, on the verge of hyperventilating.

Lexi reached toward her and did her best to sound nonchalant. "Are you kidding me? My dad could find the diamond in the refuse pile. Honest. He wouldn't need any stupid trackers. It's just the Imperium who needs them."

They reached the girl. Reeves gripped Rumi's elbow while

Lexi peeled off the watch, then tossed it on the couch. His smile vanished. "We need to go. Now."

Lexi dashed back to the bedroom, grabbed her tablet, tucked it into her backpack, and returned to the living room. "I'm ready."

He stopped her at the door. "Are you crazy? You can't take the tablet. It's too much of a risk. They can trace that too."

She shook her head as she swung the bag over her shoulders. "This will all be for nothing if we don't have the list. The only way to get the list is from the email. We've got to risk it. Besides, it'll take them a hot minute to think of the tablet *after* they realize we don't have the watches."

They exited the apartment, and she started toward the elevator before Reeves called out. "No. We need to take the stairs."

"Right. We need to find that exit."

He headed in the opposite direction, slowed with the effort of lugging Rumi. The girl walked stiff jointed like some sort of automaton.

Lexi caught up and snagged Rumi's opposite arm. Once they entered the unmonitored stairwell, they ran as fast as they could manage, Rumi acting like a third leg in a three-legged race.

The stairs seemed endless as they fumbled down them, Rumi in tow. With each level they passed without soldiers bursting through a doorway, their chances of making it out without being accosted increased.

At the ground floor, they shuffled along a corridor, doing their best to look as if they weren't running for their lives each time they passed a fellow Reclamation worker. The stench of the Reclamation floor grew with every step, so they were closing in on their target.

They slipped through a side door and encountered the workers at their stations sorting through the debris. Rumi's gagging drew Lexi's attention. If the girl's weak stomach wasn't enough to shout out that she didn't belong, her white outfit was. Might as well enroll a ballerina in a bowling competition.

Lexi hustled Rumi along the edge of the work zone, toward the locker room. "This way."

At the women's changing room, Reeves caught on. "I'll wait out here. You need to hurry."

The moment Rumi saw a toilet, she dashed into the stall and vomited. Lexi shut the door behind her, then went on a hunt for a Reclamation uniform.

By the time she found one and brought it back, Rumi stood at the sink, rinsing her mouth, her face pale. She stared at the brown jumpsuit Lexi held out to her. "I don't think I can do this."

Why do I have to get stuck with you? Lexi wouldn't say the words. "Of course you can." She gave Rumi her best winning smile. "You're already doing it. Right?"

Tears pooled in the girl's eyes.

Great. Just fantastic. "Now isn't the time to cry. You need to look like you belong here. Put it on and get moving."

Lexi pushed Rumi into the closest stall. The moment the white uniform hit the floor, Lexi stuffed it into a trash bin. While she waited, she searched for something to hide the girl's red-rimmed eyes.

When Rumi emerged, Lexi realized the brown uniform hadn't seen the inside of a washing machine since its last use. Caked-on dirt and grime made one pant leg stiff. Great. Rumi might vomit again.

Lexi slapped the hat she'd found onto Rumi's head. It hid her eyes just enough. *Perfect.* "Okay, we need to move. Try to hold it together. We're almost home free."

They exited the locker room to silence—all the machinery turned off. Giant vis screens had lowered throughout the room. Reeves nudged the girls to the side. "They just started."

The four Imperium slogans scrolled across the nearest screen while the anthem played. Lexi's nerves buzzed under her skin. She spoke close to Reeves's ear as her eyes scanned for the closest door to the outside. "I've got a bad feeling about this."

His hand clasped hers and squeezed. "Let's see if we can get to that door while everyone's focused on the vis."

Inching along the outside wall, they observed the workers as the last of the words scrolled across the screens. They were within feet of the door when Tempest Malachy's singsong voice echoed through the vast room. "Fellow citizens of the Imperium, once again, I have sobering news to share."

A video popped into the top-right corner so everyone could see Tempest speaking as the inset showed the Freedom Force marching a new captive out of an office. The camera zoomed in—on Lexi's father. A bruise bloomed around his left eye. His face filled the screen.

Her stomach fell, and her steps faltered. A squeak slipped out. He'd failed. Worse. *She'd* set him up for failure. The Imperium would murder him—because of her.

"Rumi!" Reeves released Lexi's hand and grabbed Rumi around the waist as her legs gave out. He grunted with the catch, then growled to Lexi. "We need to move. *Now.* Before someone recognizes you."

Time to woman up. You can't save him now.

The vis screen merely projected images—her father wasn't in the room with them. It didn't matter. The sense of abandoning him hit her hard as they shuffled out the door, half-dragging Rumi.

Once outside, they could watch the Imperium's propaganda on the giant vis screen built into the building cladding. Tempest's voice boomed over the two speakers flanking it. They had to be twenty feet tall. "Freedom Force members arrested a key member of the rebel group Y this morning. Sources inside the elite guard unit tell us they'll interrogate the prisoner to ferret out any accomplices. If you have any information related to this man, Gunner Verity, I encourage you to contact the department of security immediately."

"This way." Reeves's voice rose so Lexi could hear him over the speaker volume.

They scuttled around the courtyard, then out a side gate someone had left open. She'd never been so grateful for an error in security protocol. Closing the gate behind them, she paused.

The zone around the Reclamation tower had few buildings the war hadn't decimated. Roadways through the rubble ran between the Reclamation intake zone and the giant Hickory Ridge Landfill. With the workers distracted, they had a narrow opening to find a place to hide or escape to before the transport trucks took to the roads again.

"Over there." Reeves tipped his chin at a supervisor's UTV parked behind a shed. They scrambled over to it, and he checked the dashboard. "Keys are in it. Get in."

Lexi released her hold on Rumi and ran around to the passenger front seat while he manhandled Rumi into the rear seat. When she leaned as if to fall out of the open door, he pulled a seat belt across her and snapped it in place.

Then he seated himself in the driver's seat and grasped the key hanging from the ignition. "I've only driven a few times for my job, so hold on tight. Here's hoping the guy who uses this is more into the vis than his ride."

He twisted the key, and the vehicle lit up. The battery icon on the console screen showed a three-quarter charge remaining.

What good fortune. Lexi wriggled in place, urging the thing forward. "Let's go."

He backed the UTV away from the building, then pressed another pedal sending them hurtling down a well-worn path. "Where to?"

Only one building gave her any references to find Ms. Becky. The thought of returning to the place that housed the Freedom Force guards sickened her, but it would be the last place they'd think she'd go. "To the Administration building."

Chapter 23

They arrived on the outskirts of the Favela that surrounded the Administration building. Twin drones zipped down a street, headed away from them, toward the large white building in the middle of the rubble-strewn slums. Lexi looked over at Reeves, his jaw clenched, his gaze on the drones. "Should we keep the UTV? Or ditch it so we can be nimble?"

He blew out a breath and jerked his chin back at Rumi. "It's a toss-up. I'm not sure we'd be able to move fast enough with our friend here. But you're right—we can't stick to the streets either."

Lexi's heart sank. Rumi's eyes were wide, her dilated pupils black chasms to the girl's terrified soul. She stared straight ahead unblinking. Not good. "Let's stick with the vehicle as long as we can. See if you can get us closer to where we last found Ms. Becky. I'll work on this problem."

Lexi shifted in her seat, reached back, and rubbed Rumi's arm. The girl's skin was cool to the touch, and her face was so pale freckles stood out where Lexi had seen none before. "Rumi, you need to snap out of it." Lexi crooned as if trying to coax a terrified rabbit caught in a crush of the starving Favela. "Look at me. I need a little eye contact."

Rumi didn't even twitch.

Okay. The soft touch wasn't going to work. "Rumi! Snap out of it!" Lexi used the deepest, loudest tone she could muster. "We need you here, with us."

When Rumi still didn't react, Lexi gave her a small slap on the leg.

Nothing.

Lexi narrowed her eyes and muttered under her breath. "You're gonna hate me no matter what, so here goes nothing." She twisted further around in her seat to get a better reach, wrenched her hand back, then slapped Rumi's face—hard. "Snap out of it!"

The smack snapped Rumi's head to the side. When she blinked at Lexi, she cradled her hand to her blossoming cheek. Her now-focused eyes narrowed into a glare. "Ouch!"

With a grimace, Lexi popped back around to face forward. "Welcome back."

Reeves drove at a snail's pace, scanning the streets while Lexi searched the sky for the telltale drones accompanying patrols. Now, debris from a crumbling building blocked the street. He stopped at the closest intersection ahead of the mound of concrete and bricks. "We should walk from here. We can use the buildings as cover if we go through them instead of around. Someone inside one might even tell us where Ms. Becky is."

Lexi nodded and pointed to the entrance to a sketchy-looking underground garage entrance. "We can hide the UTV in there." Once they'd parked, they exited the UTV. When Rumi hesitated as if she wanted to remain with the vehicle, Lexi glared. "Need an assist to get out?"

As soon as Lexi took a step toward her, Rumi fumbled with her seat belt in a frantic move to free herself and join Reeves.

The half-crushed buildings might topple in a strong gust of wind. Still, he pointed at one aligned with the direction they needed to head. "Let's go."

Making their way through the buildings was like walking in a ghost town. Former business offices sported broken chairs, phones, and desks the poor had ransacked for anything of value. Stores held mannequins, shelving, and racks, but no hangers, clothing, or supplies. Twice feet scuttled as they flushed someone out of a hiding spot. They were never fast enough to catch anyone, and yelling out didn't seem wise.

What the war and homeless left behind was choking dust, dried-out rat carcasses, crumpled protein bar wrappers, and fallen ceiling tiles, beams, and wires.

They picked through the structures, darted across empty streets, and hurried down alleyways for at least two hours before they found the building where they had last met Ms. Becky.

They arrived at the room she'd occupied—and found it empty.

Lexi's heart sank. She ran her hands through her hair. "Now what?"

Reeves scrubbed the back of his neck. "I was afraid they'd be gone. For all we know, they're sitting in an Imperium jail, waiting for the next Freedom Force parade of prisoners on the vis screens."

A squeak came from behind Lexi. When she turned, Rumi's eyes bulged as Fletcher's giant hand clamped over her mouth.

Relief relaxed tension's tight grip on Lexi. "Fletcher. Where is everyone?"

The giant's left eyebrow twitched upward, and he nodded meaningfully down at Rumi.

How tempting to let him keep his hold over the girl's mouth. Lexi's lips quirked. But she owed the girl something—didn't she?

Reeves intervened. "You can let her loose, Fletcher. Rumi's with us."

The big guy released the red-faced girl. She sucked in air as if she hadn't been able to draw a breath in his grasp.

Rumi glared at Lexi while she crossed the room, putting both Lexi and Reeves between herself and her former captor.

Fletcher folded his powerful arms over his massive chest in his bodyguard stance. "Didn't think you'd be back. Did you get the information?"

Lexi's heartbeat ticked up its rhythm. She shed her backpack and rummaged through it for the tablet. "I'm not sure. We bolted as soon as we got my father's warning. But I have the tablet with me."

"Are you crazy?" Fletcher's explosion made Lexi want to duck for cover. "You brought Imperium electronics? The Freedom Force must know exactly where you are. I'm surprised they haven't caught you yet. They must be hoping you'll lead them to us."

Before she could find the offending device, Fletcher snatched the backpack and ran out the door.

Lexi followed, hollering after the hulk's retreating form. "We had to keep it. It must have the information Ms. Becky needs about the next retirees."

Fletcher kept running, so she continued after him with Reeves close behind. She struggled to keep the giant in sight with his long strides.

Rumi stumbled with clumsy footfalls to keep up. Lexi shook her head. *Why is she my responsibility?* She retreated, grabbed the girl's arm, and resumed her chase after Fletcher and now Reeves, dragging the girl as fast as she could. Fletcher led her by two blocks. Reeves, about half that distance. It was hard to tell from her vantage point, but as he dodged in and out of buildings and alleys, she thought she saw Fletcher holler into his watch.

Watch? Must have a way to block the tracking, but I sure hope he's got a friend on the other end of the call.

Then a UTV that looked like someone had built it in the Stone Age came from the opposite direction. Fletcher and the UTV met at the far end of a building just as Lexi and Rumi turned onto the street.

A person in the back of the UTV jumped out and flipped open the lid of a heavy-looking box in the vehicle's rear. Fletcher slammed her bag into the box, and the other man shut the lid and twisted some sort of knob.

Fletcher gulped in deep breaths while waiting for Reeves, then Lexi and Rumi, to catch up. The moment all of them arrived, the driver yelled, "Get in. We need to beat it out of here."

Taking the front seat, Fletcher jutted a thumb at the back. The bench row wasn't quite long enough to fit the three of them, so they stuffed Rumi in the middle. Lexi only had one cheek fully connected to the seat, but the run had taken all she had out of her, and she was grateful to have even that much. She held on as the driver took a zigzag route away from the city center.

The buildings grew further apart until the area must have been a farm in a former life. There had been housing subdivisions on either side of the large two-story house. They drove around the house to a barn, its door open wide. Inside, a man carrying a rifle slid the door shut behind them.

The only weapons Lexi had ever seen had been in the hands of the Freedom Force. Seeing one slung across the man's shoulders made her skin crawl.

Three people came from a room near the rear. Ms. Becky with two unfamiliar men flanking her.

Ms. Becky bustled forward. "Lexi and Reeves, so good to see you again. My sources tell me you've had an adventure."

Reeves joined Lexi beside the UTV, and Rumi gripped her arm, her breath on her neck as if Rumi were using Reeves and Lexi for a shield.

Figured.

"I see you've brought a friend." Ms. Becky waved to Rumi, then the box at the back of the UTV. "And a bit of a problem as well?"

Fletcher harrumphed. "A tablet. We got it sealed up fast as we could, but you can never be certain."

Lexi's jaw tensed at the glowers aimed her way. "Sorry. But my father may have sent the list and timing for the next batch of retirees. I didn't have time to verify. I couldn't leave it."

Ms. Becky grimaced. "Hope you're right. Let's get the tablet into a secure room and open it up."

It took both Fletcher and the driver to lift the heavy box out of the UTV. Everyone followed them to the room Ms. Becky had come from.

Beyond the rickety doorway, the small storage room smelled of oil. A tool bench lined one wall. Various implements hung on the walls, and a small engine waited on the bench, mostly disassembled, as if they'd interrupted its repair.

One guard bent to the floor and lifted the ring of an attached door. A stairwell led them underground. They carried the box single file while everyone followed.

The musty scent of earth soothed Lexi's nose, and the cooler temperatures brought goose bumps out on her arms. She rubbed them as they gathered around a table in a room big enough to contain computer equipment, a cabinet along one wall, and an executive-sized table with chairs to hold eight. In the corner, glass enclosed a room containing a desk, table, and more computer equipment. Monitors lined one wall, depicting a combination of drone footage, camera feeds from around the Favela and the farm, and one large blank screen. The glass enclosure in the corner had metal mesh running through its walls and ceiling.

Fletcher and the driver took the box into the room. The driver waved Lexi in as well.

Curious, she followed. Fletcher shut the door, blocking out the hum of the fans and other noises. When the big guy flipped a switch on the wall, Ms. Becky's voice came through a speaker in the corner. "The room you are in is sealed, but we can chat through the speakers."

The driver opened the box's heavy lid and pulled out her tablet. "Any trackers the Imperium has on electronics can't be traced in this room. We also have a secure line to the internet we can use if we need to. It'll be risky though. So let's hope the file was already on your tablet and downloaded before we brought it in here. If it was, we won't need to connect and chance a trace."

He waved her over to stand beside him, turned her tablet on, and held it out to her to unlock it with her fingerprint. Once it was open, her father's message still filled the screen, just as it had the moment they'd read it. Her stomach twisted at the words. Ignoring the sensation, she checked for the telltale symbol. "See? There *is* an attachment."

The man nodded and opened it, and she closed her eyes as the man read off what they'd both seen. "It's got a date and time and a list of the names. It's everything we needed."

Her father had done as she'd asked. He'd risked everything for her, even though he didn't believe in the rebellion. *She* had been his downfall. A tear welled, and she brushed it away before it could fall.

After pulling a cable from a drawer, the driver connected the tablet to his computer. "I'll load it onto my machine. Then we can sort through the list and see how many of these people we can convince retirement isn't real."

Her body tensed, her fingers itching to get to the keyboard herself. They needed to save as many of the retirees as they could. She wouldn't allow her father's sacrifice to be in vain.

The keyboard clicking drew her attention to the computer monitor. Driver Guy had already loaded the list. The computer digested the information as it searched a database.

A low whistle came from the driver's lips, and he handed her tablet back. "Looks like another message came in while you were on the run."

Her hands trembled as she took the tablet and opened the message. The air left her body as bile rose in her throat. Her father's battered face stared back at her from the device. Blood dribbled from his nose and one swollen-shut eye. Underneath, the message was simple.

We know what you have. If you want your father to live, turn yourself in with the list before 0800 tomorrow. Otherwise, we must use him as an example.

Chapter 24

Lexi hurled the tablet as though its message had singed her hands. It ricocheted off the desk and hit the floor. Gulping, she stared down at it, unable to control her ragged breaths. Nausea accompanied a buzz overtaking her limbs.

Knowing she could gauge her father's life expectancy in hours had been bad enough, but now she might change the outcome. *I can't make a choice like that.* "Don't make me choose." The words had come out in a croak.

Fletcher hurried over, picked up the tablet, then growled out the message to the rest of the room. "They want her to turn herself in, with the list, to save her father."

Her view dimmed, and the vision of Fletcher swam in circles. Nausea swelled, and her stomach threatened to spew.

His hands slid under her arms, lifting her. Then he plopped her into a chair.

Reeves's voice came through the speakers along with a dull thump as if he'd pounded on the thick door. "Let me in."

Fletcher dropped her tablet back into the box and shut the lid before he unlocked the door. Reeves charged through the open doorway, kneeled in front of the chair, and took her hands.

She sobbed at the sight of him, her emotions bleeding out. The promise he'd elicited was all she could think of—save herself. "I can't do it, Reeves. I can't do it."

He pressed her head to his chest. The warmth radiating from him comforted her.

"Shhh." He crooned in her ear as his hands caressed her back. "It's going to be okay. We'll figure this out like we always do—together."

Lexi focused on his blue eyes. She wanted nothing more than to get lost in them and ignore the insanity around her. How did she get so lucky as to be matched with him? Had she not failed the Imperium test, they never would have put them together. She'd never been so grateful for another human being.

Her whispered plea was for him alone, her tears laden with more than she could bear. "I can't leave him to die. If all they want is the list back, we'll just make a copy." Her voice quavered. "Right?"

The sad shake of his head and the grim line of his lips disagreed. "It doesn't matter. They want to make an example of you—along with him. No way will they let him go, Lex." He swept a teardrop from her face. "You know that."

She didn't want to believe him. There had to be a way to take back what she'd asked her father to do.

An alarm went off in the outer room. She jumped. Reeves shot to his feet. Lights strobed to the blare's beat, bathing both rooms in a sea of red. The rush of boots stomping down the stairs proceeded an armed guard who brought Ms. Becky a message. "They've found us."

Ms. Becky's face took on a determined scowl. "You know the drill. Take everything you can. We can't let any of this fall into the Imperium's hands."

Expletives flew as a flurry of activity erupted. The driver and another man ran to grab computers and other pieces of equipment while guards surrounded Ms. Becky. Fletcher dashed out of the glass enclosure and over to a cabinet that took up a quarter of one wall. When he opened it, Lexi's jaw slackened at the number and variety of guns it held. Those who weren't armed lined up to receive the weapons he handed out, including extra ammo magazines.

Gunfire erupted over their heads. The fight had moved into the barn.

Reeves queued up and accepted a rifle Lexi couldn't identify. None of the guns resembled the ones the Freedom Force issued, and the hodgepodge couldn't boast any uniformity.

Her teeth on edge, she waffled. Reeves jogged back as she stepped out of the glass room. He held out a black handgun. "Take it."

She shook her head and jammed her hands behind her back like a petulant child. "I don't know what to do with it. I might hurt someone."

He closed his eyes as if he needed to center himself. When he opened them again, his gaze had softened. "Yes, you might need to hurt someone. Especially if they intend to kill you. *Please*. You don't have to fire it unless you need to. I only want you to have the option."

Her hand trembled when she reached for the gun. It lay heavy and cool in her grip. She couldn't imagine pointing it at another human, much less pulling the trigger.

The legs of a man appeared at the top of the stairs as the explosions of gunfire drew closer to the entrance. He descended one step, then stopped, the back of his knees in view while shell casings from his weapon rained down the steps.

Fletcher handed the last man in line a weapon, then armed himself with one of the largest rifles the cabinet had held. He wrapped the strap around one shoulder and then slapped on a belt with multiple magazines. Claiming one final pistol, he hurried over to Ms. Becky and presented it to her.

She refused it. "You know I don't believe in that."

He growled, then slid it between his belt and the small of his back. "One of these days, your idealism is going to earn you a bullet between the eyes." He waved to the guards surrounding her. "Get out. Now!"

Lexi couldn't focus. She kept one eye on the stairway where the casings continued to pour down. Dividing her attention, she also watched the four guards move to the far end of the room and through a narrow doorway.

Fletcher hollered over the blaze of noise. "We've got an escape tunnel, but we don't move until the equipment is secured. Got it?"

Reeves joined him in a column ready to ascend the stairway.

Then Fletcher ordered, "Kill the lights."

The strobing red beacon died along with the rest of the lights, plunging them into darkness. The only light now came from the stairway and the tunnel doorway.

The man who'd been firing on the stairway tumbled backward down the remaining steps and collapsed in a bloody heap. The fall twisted his neck at such an unnatural angle, he must be dead.

A man further back in the room started toward the stairs as if he planned to replace the fallen soldier. Fletcher stopped his advance with an arm. "Stand firm. The entrance is a fatal funnel to anyone who tries to come down those steps. We'll defend from here." Then he shouted behind him, never taking his focus off the open staircase. "All right, you heartbreakers, we can hold this, but you need to get that equipment out of here." He then let loose a barrage of bullets up and out of the stairway opening. "When they start through the door, gift them pain."

Reeves's lips flattened into grim determination. Then he pivoted to Lexi. "Follow Ms. Becky. The guards will keep you safe."

"No way!" Fletcher's bark caused her to jump—a feat over the din of the men firing upward. "Every person—every gun—gets focused on that entrance until cleanup is complete. *Then* the rest of us follow."

Reeves's glare could have melted granite, but it had no effect on its intended target who returned the look with a guttural growl.

Not wanting to cause a fight between the two men, she sidled up between Reeves and Fletcher and pointed her gun barrel toward the opening above the stairway. She directed her next words to Reeves. "I'm fine. I can help."

Fletcher harrumphed, reached over to her gun, and flipped a switch on it. "It works best if you take the safety off."

Her face warmed. How in the world could she have known anything about how guns worked? It wasn't as if they'd had a class in school on the subject. She aimed at the stairway, the same as the rest of the team, and pulled the trigger. The kick of the gun shocked her and knocked her backward a foot. She growled, stepped back into the line, aimed, and fired again.

Meanwhile, men clambered to collect the last of the hardware and shove it into the metal security boxes. Her former driver dropped in laptops, a drone, a helmet, and a controller. Two other men grabbed it by the handles and hustled through the back door.

A man with curly hair opened a backpack. A stack of strange off-white clay bricks lay in the center with wires coming out of them.

She refocused on the entryway, firing off two more shots. Her heart stopped its furious pace when, in her peripheral view, Reeves collapsed. "No!" Dropping to her knees beside him, she forced down nausea as blood flowed down the side of his face and head. "Reeves… *Reeves*."

His eyes didn't focus as he moaned.

Too much blood. There was too much blood. She couldn't lose him. Not now.

All the things she hadn't told him… How much she needed him. How much she… loved him. Did she love him? Bent on refusing anything the Imperium had arranged, she neglected to give him—and her—a chance for genuine love. A sob broke through her thoughts. She pressed her hands over the wound, stemming the flow, while the battle continued to rage. She had to get him to the tunnel—to safety. Scanning the room, she begged for attention. "Help us!"

Fletcher glanced her way before refocusing on the stairway. "Get him out of here."

As Fletcher fired another barrage of bullets, two men lifted Reeves under the arms and dragged him toward the tunnel. Her stomach clenched at his groans. She'd switch places in a heartbeat. Determined to keep going, she snatched her gun off the floor, tucked it into her waistband, and trailed them. His sticky blood covered everything she touched.

The man kneeling by the backpack with the bricks flipped a

switch and called out, "It's ready to go."

Fletcher nodded, then shouted at his men. "Down the tunnel."

Half the men sprinted toward the passageway exit while the rest backed away from the entrance to the basement, firing intermittently.

Lexi followed the men who dragged Reeves away. She stopped before going through the door.

Where was Rumi? Her gaze darted around the fast-emptying room. Where could that girl have gone? Then two men grasped either side of a metal box that had been stacked on top of another near the back exit. Rumi popped up from behind it, her eyes wide and tear-filled.

That girl was going to get herself killed. Rumi's hands covered her ears, and tears streamed down her face.

Lexi grabbed Rumi's arm. "Come on!"

The tunnel's musty air smelled of earth, though Lexi couldn't make out in the dim lighting if they were walking on a dirt path. She hurried to catch up to the men who had Reeves. There had been so much blood. What if he had lost too much? She shook her head. No—she wouldn't allow the thought.

They must have jogged a few hundred yards before the light grew brighter near the front of their snaking formation. When they drew closer, the ceiling opened above a thick set of wooden steps, almost a glorified ladder.

Once they'd climbed the stairs, they gathered in a ghost of a former forest. Dead, blackened trees surrounded them, the ground just as devoid of life. Distant drones drew her attention to the backside of the barn. She could still make out more than a dozen drones buzzing above and around it. She was grateful for the cover of the skeleton wood, though leaves on the trees would have provided better cover.

The gunfire from the barn silenced. Then a bullhorn echoed through the trees. "Lexi Verity. If you come out now, we'll let the rest of the rebels go."

More shots rang out back at the barn. Then the ground shook beneath her feet. She shuddered as a mammoth orange ball of fire bloomed where the barn had stood. Her knees turned to gelatin. No one could have survived that.

A moan behind her brought her attention back to the living. She rushed to where the men had set Reeves down, his back propped up against a tree. One man had wrapped something around his head and pressed Reeves's bloody hand against the bandage.

She ran and fell to her knees beside him. "Is he going to be okay?"

"The bullet just grazed him. Head wounds bleed like a witch. Makes it look worse than it is." The man rose. "Keep pressure on it for now. The bleeding will let up. I need to go help the team. I'll check on him later."

After the guy walked away, she put her hand over Reeves's. His face was too pale. Her heart ached to make everything right again. "You scared me. I thought you were going to die."

He gave her a crooked grin. "Nah. Nothing like that. Just wanted a cool-looking scar."

His flippant response released the dam building inside of her. She flung her arms around him in a tight embrace and laughed as tears flowed down her face. "You're going to end up with half of a lopsided mohawk."

He reached his bloody hand toward her and swiped at her wet cheek. "As long as I still get to be with you, I don't care what I look like."

Her lips quivered, and tears obscured her vision. "Oh, Reeves." If he could flirt, he was going to be fine. She bent her head down and brushed her lips against his, reveling in the touch of his warmth against her. His shocked look would have made her laugh if they weren't about to be blown to smithereens.

In a flurry behind them, the armed guards kept Ms. Becky in the center of their formation, backs to her, guns trained outward, like the stabilizers keeping an airbridge aloft.

Fletcher led a group of men as they uncovered several UTVs. Rumi shadowed him as if he were her lifeline. The moment the first one was in the open, the guards walked Ms. Becky over and put her in the rear seat. Two of the armed men flanked her while another took the front seat, along with the driver. A fourth strapped himself to a makeshift seat in the rear cargo bed, facing backward.

They paused while the rest of the team got situated.

"Come on. Let's go." Lexi helped Reeves to his feet. At first, he seemed unsteady, so she helped him into one vehicle's passenger side.

Rumi had already clambered into the back seat while Lexi claimed the driver's spot. She'd seen how Reeves operated the vehicle. How hard could it be? "Where do you think we're going?"

Reeves winced, keeping his hand pressed to the bandage now drenched in red. "Any place in the opposite direction of the Imperium works for me."

A vehicle loaded with armed men took the lead. The UTV with Ms. Becky followed. The rest trailed in as rapid a fashion as they could. Reeves must have seen the panic creeping into Lexi's heart as she tried to remember the sequences he'd used to maneuver the vehicle. "The vertical pedal is your accelerator," he explained. "It makes you move in the direction the shifter says you're headed. You're in park right now. Press the horizontal pedal whenever you need to stop or change the shifter. Depress it now and move the shifter to D for drive, then press the accelerator."

She followed his instructions, and the vehicle leaped forward, whipping their heads backward with the momentum. Reeves let out a low moan.

"Sorry."

Their original driver held a drone remote and adjusted the knobs as the UTV he rode in sped ahead of them. She searched the sky but couldn't see clearly through the tangle of dead tree limbs.

The road through the woods seemed like nothing more than widened animal trails. Though the seat belts kept them from flying out at every rock and dip they powered over, she used one hand to cling to the roll cage while the other steered.

The trees had thinned out when they exited the woods near what must have once been a housing development. Cratered roadways snaked through the rubble. Nothing grew in the dirt, as if whatever bomb dropped on it had polluted even the soil. While they moved along, the vehicles ahead kicked dust high into the air. It coated their faces and invaded their mouths and eyes. Lexi released the roll cage and squinted with a hand up to shield her eyes.

A drone whirred high above the lead UTV. Then something whistled overhead and slammed into the drone, reducing it to bits of flame. *Not good.*

She glanced back. A fleet of Imperium drones headed their way. Freedom Force UTVs wouldn't be far behind. They were too exposed. There had to be some place to take cover. Where?

Burned-out woods lay to the left beyond the decimated homes. To the right rose the skeletons of a city with huge crumbling pillars that might have been bridges of some sort, their decks smashed flat. Ahead, a dust cloud billowed toward them.

A closer view revealed several vehicles generated the dirt storm. Were they about to get sandwiched between known foes and the unknown? How much worse could this get?

She leaned toward Reeves. "If that's another Imperium troop, we'll never make it to the woods in time."

Another flock of drones preceded the dust cloud, passed over the rebel group, and fired on the Imperium's flying fleet, dropping them one at a time even as they suffered their own losses.

"They're on our side." She allowed herself a tentative smile. "Someone has come to our rescue."

Reeves let out a grunt. "Let's hope we aren't jumping out of a frying pan and into a fire."

The dust bowl swirled closer, a UTV in the lead. Armed men occupied the seats—another stood in the rear cargo bed. Her heart rose into her throat as the two forces drove at full speed toward each other, the moment of truth drawing closer by the second.

Then the people in the opposing force gave hand signals, their thumbs and pinkies flying high with the other three fingers curled under in the shape of a *Y*. Dirt coated their faces, and goggles protected their eyes. Their vehicles kicked choking tornadoes of dirt into the air. They passed by, enormous guns strapped to the tops of the roll cages, ready to engage at the first sign of their enemy.

She let out a whoop.

Reeves grinned at her, his teeth almost florescent in contrast to his filthy face.

Behind them, a firefight broke out. Or so she assumed with gunfire fierce, but visibility minimal. The rapid-fire machine-gun reports drifted further away as they continued their progress forward. Perhaps the Imperium forces were retreating. She could hope, though she wasn't about to slow down to find out.

On the far side of the former subdivision, the lead UTV slowed to a stop. Each successive vehicle followed suit until they'd all gathered in a circle. Ms. Becky alighted while her entourage surrounded her, searching the horizon in all directions for whatever might come next.

Lexi and Reeves joined the rebels, facing the direction from which they'd just come. The fighting sounds had ended. A new cloud of dust headed toward them again. Soon, the group of UTVs stopped nearby. A man too large to fit through a normal door without ducking exited the lead vehicle and lumbered toward them, the rifle in his hands not aimed at them. He could have been Fletcher's twin.

Reeves stepped in front of Lexi and edged her behind him, acting as a shield. He leaned back and whispered. "Stay behind me. If anything funny happens, get back in the UTV and take off. Don't wait for me."

Right. As if she'd leave him to face this questionable-looking group. Especially after the head wound he'd suffered. She let hope flow through her body since the unit had rescued them. She nudged his shoulder. "Who do you think they are?"

He shrugged. "Watch and see."

Ms. Becky and her team pushed through. Then she parted

the two forward-facing guards to address the hulking giant. "Thrym. It's good to see you again."

The brute held up a hand, and a slight feminine figure ran from a vehicle in the far back, then stopped short of Ms. Becky. Something about her gait seemed familiar, but Lexi couldn't quite place it. A layer of dirt hid her facial features. When she plucked her goggles off, her eyes searched the group as if expecting to find someone.

The moment Lexi saw the woman's eyes, she knew who she was and who she was looking for. She rushed around Reeves and ran full tilt toward the woman whose eyes went wide. They collided in a crushing embrace. "Mom!"

Chapter 25

L exi could have rested in her mother's embrace for the rest of her life. After what seemed like only seconds, her mother pushed Lexi to arm's length and stared into her eyes. The dirt on her face, mixed with trailing tears, had turned into mini rivers of mud.

When Mom smiled, her teeth flashed like white beacons in a dark void. She laughed. "You're a mess."

Though the tears left her voice husky, Lexi couldn't help but join in the laughter. "You don't look any better."

A hand gripped Lexi's waist, and someone cleared his throat. Reeves stood there, his face grim as if something were bothering him. "Is it too soon for an introduction?"

In the moment's insanity, she'd forgotten he was there. She nudged him around to stand beside her and entwined her fingers with his, the spark of chemistry between them warming her. Then she put her hand into her mother's and smiled into the eyes she thought she'd never see again. "Mom, this is my husband, Reeves." She squeezed his hand. "And this is my mom."

Reeves stuck out a bloody hand. "Pleasure to meet you, Mrs. Verity."

Ms. Becky and her armed groupies moved in and joined

their gathering. "Tora, I can't say I'm not happy to see you again. We especially appreciate the rescue." Also grim-faced, she continued. "I *am* shocked to see you alive, though. Care to explain why we all thought you were dead?"

Reeves nodded with Ms. Becky's question, crossing his arms over his chest. "We'd all love to hear that answer."

Stunned that he'd be so bold, Lexi hissed at him. *"Reeves."*

Opposing emotions warred in her heart. Part of her didn't want to question anything about her mother's reappearance, as if asking the questions might cause her mother to vanish into the ether.

The more she thought about it, though, the more she needed to hear the answer. To understand why she'd been abandoned by the one person she thought loved her more than anything.

Her mother's face remained impassive until she looked at Lexi. Then she swallowed hard, and something glimmered in her eyes. "Your grandparents are waiting to meet you in Solitude."

Lexi's heart flipped. "Nana and Gramps? But... I thought... isn't Solitude a lie?" She wrapped her free hand around Reeves's arm, still gripping tight to his hand with the other, needing confirmation she wasn't crazy. "I don't understand."

Both hands held upward, Mom's eyes pleaded with her. Who was this woman Lexi thought she'd known? She backed away and leaned into Reeves, the only person she could rely on.

He pulled her in, her back tight against the warmth of his chest as they faced her mother together. "I get the feeling your mother's disappearance relates to your grandparents' retirement."

Fletcher harrumphed behind Ms. Becky. Ms. Becky stepped closer to Lexi's mother, challenging her with a glare.

"We built Y upon the teachings of Yeshua. We're a pacifist organization. But a group of warmongers tried to sway our youngest members. To convict them of the need to use violence to solve our problems." Arms across her chest, Ms. Becky raised her chin. "Lexi, your mother was my right hand in rescuing the retirees and keeping them safe and fed in the Favela. Until that wasn't enough for her. It seems she's joined the other side. Chose violence over peace."

Lexi's mother spat on the ground at Ms. Becky's feet. "Peace? You call the way our people die of starvation *peace*? You call the ones we can't get to before the Imperium 'retires' them *peace*? How is *any* of that peaceful?" Her glare seared Lexi, then softened. "It's already a war. Y just isn't fighting back. The defeat has already occurred. Only Ms. Becky hasn't realized it yet."

She waved in the air around them. "You're a bunch of cowards."

The two women stood toe to toe as if daring each other to say the next word.

Then Ms. Becky stepped back. "Was Yeshua a coward? I don't think so."

Who was this Yeshua person? But that question must wait. Lexi touched her mother's arm to pull her attention away from the unspoken battle between these women. "They have Dad."

Mom's shoulders slumped. "I know. I'm sorry. Is it true that he joined the rebellion?"

A lump clogged Lexi's throat. Somehow, she must force the confession past it. "I forced him to help. He did it for me."

Her mother covered Lexi's hand on her arm, her touch warm, familiar—a lifetime of comfort coursing through it. "Your father and I never agreed on most things, so it's hard to imagine he would have joined our cause."

Thrym stepped up behind Mom. "Sorry to cut the reunion short, but we need to get out of the open. The Freedom Force will send reinforcements."

Mom nodded. "Ms. Becky, it would be safest if you returned to Solitude with us. You'll be impressed with what we've put together. Once things settle down, assuming they do, we can escort you back to the Favela."

Solitude. Her grandparents. Lexi couldn't wait to see them again. As they all filed back to their vehicles, her heart floated as if someone had filled it with helium.

Though she tried to get there first, Reeves took the driver's seat, a stony grimace on his face. She didn't have it in her to argue. They drove in the line of UTVs heading away from the Imperium.

Lexi had only been outside an Imperium building a few times in her life. She'd never seen the destruction of the war. They passed through decimated cities, up and down hills with burned stumps that had been trees in a time long past. Even the rocks showed blackened and fractured surfaces.

No matter how rough the ride, Rumi sat silent in the back seat, rubbing her hand up and down her shoulder belt, her eyes boring holes in the back of Reeves's head.

It had grown dark by the time they crested a hill and lights glowed in the distance. Reeves checked the console. "I'd hoped to see some sort of civilization soon. There's not much left in the battery. We'll end up walking if that isn't our destination."

More signs of habitation came into view as they dipped into a valley. A river meandered through what must have been a farm. Lexi's heart did a quick tap dance. There were live trees in the valley. Honest-to-goodness trees—with leaves and everything.

They crossed over a bridge that spanned the river and entered civilization. A two-story white farmhouse with peeling paint almost glowed at the center of dozens of tents. Floodlights on the corners of its roof lit the immediate area. Armed guards walked a fence surrounding the makeshift town. A firepit sparked into the air as they passed through a group of tents. Laughter floated from the people gathered around the blaze.

The line of UTVs slowed closer to the farmhouse. Most were elderly people. Some much older than her grandparents.

The thought of Nana and Gramps had her scanning the crowd. All the gray hair and wrinkles gave her hope Y's rebel army had rescued more than had died in recent years.

The parade ended at the front steps of a wraparound porch connected to an enormous home. Armed men lined the deck.

Lexi's mom alighted from the lead vehicle and ran to the front door. She rushed through the doorway without closing it. They all followed, grateful to be done with their long, dirty ride through the devastation.

When Lexi's feet hit the ground, its spongy texture cushioned them. She looked down. Grass. Everywhere in the glow surrounding the house, a mat of green plants thrived. There was so much plant life here they *walked* on the stuff. Her mouth hung open as she kneeled to run her hands across the lush carpet.

This must be paradise.

A screech brought her attention back to the front door, and she forgot the greenery and ran to meet her nana. Squeals filled the porch as they hugged and swayed in a sort of dance. Lexi breathed in her nana's perfume. By the time they parted, tears streamed down both their faces.

Nana wiped her cheeks with her shirtsleeve. "Oh, baby girl. We've missed you so much."

A gruff throat clearing erupted near the door. Just inside the entryway, Gramps sat in a wheelchair with Mom behind him. Lexi dashed over and bent to hug him. She'd squeezed Nana with fervor, but Gramps looked too frail for more than a gentle embrace. When she eased back, his eyes glistened. She gave him a peck on the cheek. "Love you, Gramps."

Nana came up behind Lexi and wrapped an arm around her shoulders while Lexi held Gramps's shaky hand.

Mom tipped her chin. "I think someone wants to meet your grandparents."

Reeves had stepped up and stood, hands in pockets, waiting.

Lexi laughed and hauled Reeves into the group. "Nana, Gramps—this is Reeves. My husband."

Gramps held out a quivering hand. "Welcome to the family, son."

Grasping the wrinkled hand with his, Reeves smiled down at his grandfather-in-law. "A pleasure to meet you, sir."

Wet coughs spasmed out of Gramps. Mom wheeled him back into the house while they followed. Once the door was closed, Mom patted Gramps's arm. "That's enough excitement for one day."

Gramps reached for Nana's hand. "I guess it's time for bed."

Nana gave Lexi one last embrace. "We'll talk more in the morning." Then she rolled Gramps's wheelchair around and headed out of the room.

A timid knock rasped against the front door. When Mom opened it, Rumi stood there, her eyes big and head hanging like a lost puppy. She stared past Mom, searching the room.

"Lexi?"

Guilt hit. In the reunion's excitement, she'd forgotten the girl. "Here." She walked over and scooped an arm around Rumi. A bundle of nerves twisted in her gut. "Mom, this is Rumi."

"No need to explain." Her mother seemed to sense Lexi's discomfort. "We have our sources inside the Imperium's headquarters. I know who this young lady is and to whom she's married."

Rumi's cheeks burned. "Thank you for saving us."

They stood staring at each other.

When Lexi bit her bottom lip, uncertain of what to do, Reeves saved her. "Is there a tent or someplace we can get some rest? It's been a full day." He touched his bandaged head. "And I'm not feeling all that great."

"Of course, you all must be exhausted." Mom pointed toward the stairway. "There are plenty of guest rooms. We'll assign you all tents tomorrow. We use the house as a headquarters. New arrivals bunk here for the first night."

She led them to the second floor and down the hallway to the right. Ms. Becky and her security team went to the left. Mom stopped at the first door and opened it. "This one's for you and Reeves." She pointed Rumi further down the hallway. "I've got a smaller room on the end for you. It was a nursery in a prior life, but it holds a single bed frame just fine. You'll be snug as a bug in there."

Reeves waved Lexi into their room. "After you."

A huge oak bed lay along one wall, a matching dresser on another. The room offered nothing besides the bedding. Even the walls were bare except for the champagne paint.

Lexi toed the threadbare carpet. "At least it isn't white."

Someone knocked on the doorframe. A woman with long gray hair, blue eyes, and a handful of linens stood in the doorway. "There's a bathroom two doors down. Shared with everyone on this side of the house, so don't dawdle. I've got towels for you, as well as some clothes we thought might fit. I'm sure you'll want a shower before bed."

Reeves accepted the proffered pile and set it atop the dresser. Then he closed the door as the woman retreated down the hallway. "You get your shower first. I can wait. While you're in there, I'll see if I can scrounge up something to eat and drink."

Her chest swelled, even as she resisted scratching at the grime clinging to her. "Thank you."

Within an hour, they'd both bathed and dressed in black T-shirts and loose black joggers. Each had a protein bar, along with tall glasses of water. Reeves sported a fresh bandage.

Lexi crawled into the bed while he switched off the light before joining her. At first, they both lay face up, staring at the ceiling. Then she squirmed closer and snuggled as he curved her into him.

She sighed, her arm slung over his waist. She breathed in his scent mixed in with the smell of the soap he'd used—like fresh lemons.

They were safe. Her father wasn't—but she forced that thought out of her mind. That would be first on her agenda in the morning.

"Reeves..." Her voice quivered with emotion she hadn't felt before. "When I saw you lying on the ground, covered in blood, I–I realized something." She lifted her head and turned sideways, leaning on her elbow. "The Imperium might have put us together based on some stupid test, but..." She licked her lips, unsure how to express her feelings. "I've come to realize you really are my soul mate."

She let out a short laugh as she tucked a strand of her hair behind her ears. "I've always wanted to fall in love like people used to before the Imperium. I've never liked the idea of being told who to marry." Her lips quirked. "As I'm sure you well know. I guess what I'm trying to say is... I will forever be grateful I botched my test. Because if I hadn't..." She traced the line of his strong jaw, emotion welling inside her chest. "I'd have never met you."

His firm hand cupped her face, and she leaned into it, reveling in his strength. "I'm glad too, Lexi. You're the most powerful girl—er, woman—I've ever met. And if I had to be married with someone so strong-willed and bent on changing the course of history..." He tweaked her chin. "I sure am glad I married you."

She rested her head on his chest again, her arms wrapped around his waist. "Do you know what tomorrow is?"

His breath was warm on her cheek as he leaned in toward her. "No. What day is tomorrow?"

A giggle escaped before she could spit it out. "It's the last day of our honeymoon."

She could almost feel his big grin before he tipped her chin. He tightened his hold on her and feathered kisses along her cheek until their lips joined in a deepened kiss. Heart pounding, she wondered if their match had resulted from some type of cosmic intervention—because his kisses definitely felt out of this world.

A slow smile stretched up her lips as she laid her head back down on his chest.

"Hmm." His chest rumbled against her cheek when he spoke.

"I hope we get to enjoy at least that one day in peace."
She closed her eyes, exhausted. "Me too."